A Brighter Tomorrow

My Journey with Julie

by Megan McDonald

⭐ American Girl®

For Jordana

Beforever

Beforever is about making connections.
It's about exploring the past, finding your
place in the present, and thinking about the
possibilities your future can bring. And it's about
seeing the common thread that ties girls from
all times together. The inspiring characters you
will meet stand up for what they care about
most: Helping others. Protecting the earth.
Overcoming injustice. Through their courageous
stories, discover how staying true to your own
beliefs will help make your world better
today—and tomorrow.

A Journey Begins

This book is about Julie, but it's also about a girl like you who travels back in time to Julie's world. You, the reader, get to decide what happens in the story. The choices you make will lead to different journeys and new discoveries.

When you reach a page in this book that asks you to make a decision, choose carefully. The decisions you make will lead to different endings. (Hint: Use a pencil to check off your choices. That way, you'll never read the same story twice.)

Want to try another ending? Read the book again—and then again. Find out what happens to you and Julie when you make different choices.

Before your journey ends, take a peek into the past, on page 138, to discover more about Julie's time.

onk honk, beep beep beep! This city noise is so loud! I shut the window and curl onto the window seat, the only part of my room that feels like home in our new apartment. I had a window seat in my old room at our house in Ohio. We just moved to this apartment in San Francisco a week ago, and I'm still getting used to the view outside my window. Through the leafy treetops I can see a whole row of colorful Victorian houses like ours, painted in pastel colors. Back in Ohio, houses are mostly white or beige; here in San Francisco, they are yellow and pink and blue and sometimes even lavender, with fancy trim that looks like frosting on a cake. My mom, who's an architect, says these homes are called Painted Ladies. They do sort of look like ladies all dressed up.

Closing my eyes for a moment, I imagine the view from my window seat back in Ohio. There's the old buckeye tree on our front lawn, with the tire swing just big enough to fit me and my best friend, Chloe, who lived right next door to me. If I concentrate hard enough, I can almost hear my dad singing oldies in the kitchen as he prepares my favorite breakfast: banana chocolate-chip pancakes.

"What're you doing?" My little brother's voice snaps me out of my daydream.

"Ever heard of knocking?" I ask him. Zack's only seven, but that's old enough to understand about privacy.

Zack shrugs. "It was open." He flops down on my bed and twirls a section of his curly brown hair just above his ear with his fingers. He does that whenever he's feeling anxious about something. Lately he does it a lot.

"Zack, you're going to get a bald spot. Pretty soon you'll be as bald as Dad!"

Zack swallows. "I miss Dad," he says. "I want to go home."

"Zack, we've been over this a gazillion times," I tell him. "This *is* home now. And Dad will be here before you know it." But I understand how Zack feels. I don't think this little apartment in the middle of California will ever feel like home.

It's bad enough that Mom and Dad sold our house in Ohio, the only house Zack and I have ever known. Even worse is that today is Saturday, the day that Chloe and I always meet in the front yard for our

Super Saturday Sillyfest—which usually means we do a crazy dance or tell funny jokes. Worst of all is that Dad is still in Ohio and we might not see him till Christmas.

Ever since Dad lost his job over six months ago, he and Mom have been arguing more than usual. When Mom got the job offer in California, my parents decided that Dad would stay in Ohio to take some computer training courses so that he can find a good job when he moves to San Francisco. Mom told us it was a good time for them to "take a little vacation from each other."

Zack starts twirling his hair again. "I hate it here," he says, his face tightening. I can tell that he's trying not to cry. "Are Mom and Dad going to get a divorce?"

I pretend I didn't hear him and act as if I'm looking at something really interesting outside. I don't like to talk about these things, and I *really* don't like to think about the *D* word: divorce.

My mind flashes back to the moment we drove away from our house with the tire swing. Zack cried as he watched Dad fade into the distance, waving. Mom tried to reassure us that things are going to

work out just fine. Zack looked at me with a face that seemed to say, *Do you think so, too?* I just stuffed ear-buds in my ears and listened to my music. I wanted to tell him that yes, things will work out, but I didn't know if they will. I still don't.

Zack throws a pillow at me. "Did you hear me? I asked if Mom and Dad—"

"Look, Zack!" I say, pointing out the window and trying to avoid his question. "A bulldog! You love bulldogs!"

He doesn't budge. He wipes his cheek with the back of his hand and gazes at me with a hard look in his eyes. "Why won't you talk to me?" he asks. "Do you like it here?"

Of course not! I want to tell him. *I'm just as sad as you!* But I don't say it, because Zack's depending on me to be the big sister. And isn't a big sister supposed to stay strong and pretend that everything is fine? Besides, what does Zack know? He's just a little kid.

I relax my shoulders and give him a forced smile. "You know what? Let's go get some of those mini muffins that you love at that coffee shop downstairs. And a chocolate shake!"

Zack heaves a sigh. "Just forget it," he mumbles, and shuffles out of my room.

A warm tear rolls down my cheek. I think about going after him and telling him how I really feel, but then I hear the little jingle on my laptop that signals a call on video chat.

❀ *Turn to page 6.*

It's Chloe! I pull the computer onto my lap.

"Hey, Chlo-coa Puff!" I squeal when her face appears on my screen. As usual, she's wearing her favorite daisy barrettes to pull back her curly red hair. No matter what, she's always wearing a flower.

"Hiya, Hula Hoop!" she replies, using the nickname she gave me for my special basketball move. "I sure wish you were here."

"Me too," I say. "Saturday doesn't seem nearly as silly without you."

Chloe crosses her eyes, sticks out her tongue, and puffs her cheeks out.

"I take it back!" I say with a laugh. "What are you going to do today?"

She tells me about a birthday party for one of our friends. "We're going to make cupcakes and frost them ourselves. I'm going to make a big pretty flower on mine."

That's my Chloe, I think. *Flowers on everything.*

"Sounds like you guys are going to have a lot of fun," I say, trying to give her my best I'm-happy-for-you smile.

"It won't be the same without you," she says earnestly. "How's your new school? You haven't found a

new best friend to replace me yet, have you?"

"Get real, Chloe. Nobody will even look at me at school. It's like I'm wearing a big neon sign over my head that says WEIRDO." I can't bring myself to tell how close to the truth this is. Just yesterday, I walked around during the entire lunch hour with a sign taped to my back that said "WALKING FREAK SHOW." I wore it all the way into social studies class, and I wouldn't have known about it all day if it weren't for a quiet girl named Savannah who pulled it off and showed it to me.

"I'm sure it will get better," Chloe assures me. "Does your school have a basketball team? You should try out. Maybe you could make some friends on the team."

"Yeah, there's a team, but they're really good. They, like, win championships and stuff." I was a pretty good player on our fourth-grade team in Ohio, but I don't think I could play nearly as well without Chloe and the rest of my teammates. I'm about to tell her this when I notice the time on my laptop. "It's 12:34! Quick, close your eyes and make a wish!"

We both squeeze our eyes closed. My wish is for my dad to come home and everything to feel normal again.

I hear Chloe's mom calling her name in the background. Chloe huffs. "I've got to go. I have a *ton* of chores to get done before the birthday party."

I wish I could go with her to the party so badly it hurts. My eyes even start to sting. But all I say is, "Have a great party, Chlo-coa Puff. Say hi to everyone for me."

"Will do! See you later, alligator," she says, giving our traditional telephone sign-off.

"After a while, crocodile," I reply. "Time to go, buffalo."

"See you soon, raccoon." She waves and hangs up.

I pick up my computer and place it on my desk before slumping heavily back onto the window seat. The cushion shifts under me, and as I reach down to adjust it, I feel some hinges where the seat meets the wall. Does the seat open? I toss the cushion onto my bed, and sure enough, the bench seat is hinged. I lift up the lid and peer inside, then reach my hand in and fish around. Among the dust and icky cobwebs, I find a dangly peace-sign earring, a nail clipper, a rainbow hair ribbon, and a half-dollar from 1975 with a picture of President Kennedy on it. It's as if I've found a time capsule!

Standing up, I tie the rainbow ribbon around my

ponytail and put the other treasures in my pocket. I'm about to close the lid when something shiny catches my eye in the corner of the open window seat. A marble? A button? No, it's a ring, with a big black stone. I pick it up and close the window seat to sit down. I slip on the ring, and as I admire it on my hand, the stone begins to lighten in color. Is it one of those mood rings? Just then, the room starts to spin. I close my eyes, trying to make it stop. Then my stomach drops and I feel as if I'm falling. I land with a thud and open my eyes.

Oddly, I'm still sitting on the window seat—but everything has changed. The room looks like my room, but all my stuff has been replaced with someone else's. Beaded curtains and a scalloped canopy hang around the bed, which is covered by a colorful bedspread. Next to the bed is a chair in the shape of a giant egg and a matching ottoman. A lava lamp sits on the desk, next to an old-fashioned record player and tape recorder. On the dresser is a framed picture of a family: two parents, a teenage girl, and a girl around my age. That girl has long blonde hair with a little braid down one side and sparkly dark-brown eyes. A second photo shows the same blonde girl with her arm around the shoulder

of a pretty Asian girl. Alphabet stickers decorate the border of the photo, spelling out JULIE + IVY = BEST FRIENDS. Could this be that blonde girl's room?

How did I get here? I was sitting on the window seat in my new room one moment and then—*whoosh*—I ended up in this strange place. Did I fall down some sort of rabbit hole like in *Alice in Wonderland*? I return to the window and open the seat to peek inside. Weird—now it's filled to the brim with books and stuffed animals. I don't think I could possibly have fallen through there! I close the lid and sit down, confused. Across the street, I see a house painted bright purple with turquoise trim, but I swear when I looked out this window just a few minutes ago it was painted green with white trim. Even the trees seem different—a lot smaller. This morning, I could hardly see the green house through the canopy of tree branches. Now the trees are just spindly little things that hardly take up any room on the sidewalk.

I glance down at the mood ring, which has turned a cloudy amber color. It seemed almost as if the . . . transformation, or whatever it was, happened when I put on the ring. I slip it off, and suddenly I'm spin-

ning again, as if I'm turning cartwheels. Then, just as suddenly, the spinning stops, and I'm back in my own room again. My old desk, my star quilt on my bed, my unpacked boxes. I look out the window—and just as I remembered, the house across the street *is* green and white, not purple and turquoise.

The clock on my laptop says 12:35. I blink in confusion. It's been at least five minutes since Chloe and I made a wish together, and yet . . . I open my hand and stare at the ring in my palm. Is it really a mood ring? It sure seems to do more than show moods—it shows other places! What will happen if I put the ring on again? I just *have* to try it. Slipping the ring on, I feel the spinning sensation again.

Thunk! I peek with one eye. Sure enough, I'm back in that strange room with the purple house across the street.

❁ *Turn to page 12.*

I decide to explore this strange world beyond the bedroom. Like the girl's room, the rest of the apartment is just like our new San Francisco home, but Mom's sleek, modern furniture has been replaced by cool, retro stuff. In the kitchen, there's a clock in the shape of a cat whose tail and eyes move back and forth with every tick and tock. In the living room, there are beaded lampshades and ceramic pots and knotted rope plant hangers full of plants.

As I go from room to room, I feel like Goldilocks exploring the three bears' house. I suddenly realize that if somebody came home right now, I would have no way to explain how I got here! I had better get out of here before that happens.

As I step onto the sidewalk, I notice a van parked nearby on which someone has painted FLOWER POWER in colorful, swirly letters. A teenage boy with long, shaggy hair and a tie-dyed shirt leans against the van, bouncing a beanbag off of his shoe. A woman with a puffy velvet cap, a leather vest, and a long skirt passes me on the street. She smiles at me and holds up her fingers in a peace sign.

Apparently it wasn't just my room, the apartment,

and the house across the street that changed when
I put on the ring. It was the whole neighborhood—
maybe even all of San Francisco!

Feeling disoriented, I look up at our apartment
building. It's definitely the same building on the
corner of Redbud and Frederick that Mom, Zack, and
I just moved into. At least the street signs have the
same names. I look to see if the coffee shop below
our apartment is there, but just as I suspected, it isn't.
Instead there's a little boutique with a sign above the
door that says *Gladrags*.

A little bell jingles as I step into the shop. It must
be some kind of vintage thrift store. There are retro
clothes on the racks, purses made out of old blue
jeans, and colorful beaded belts. Wooden bowls on the
counter are filled with rings and bracelets made out of
silver forks and spoons! An old-fashioned boom box
sits on a shelf, playing a song I remember hearing on
Dad's favorite oldies station.

A woman about my mom's age gives me a warm
smile as she helps a customer at the cash register. She
looks vaguely familiar—and then I realize she's the
woman in the framed photo on the dresser upstairs.

"Welcome to Gladrags," she says. "Feel free to have a look around."

"Thanks," I say. I pretend to study a display of seashell night-lights as I try to figure out what's going on. How did I get here? And why?

Just then, a girl with long blonde hair pops up from behind the counter and greets me with a big smile. It's the girl from the photos on the dresser.

"Hi," the blonde girl says.

The woman at the register clears her throat and gestures in my direction. "Julie, why don't you see if our customer needs help finding anything?"

"Oh, right!" the girl says. She scurries around the counter with a basketball under her arm. "I'm Julie. Julie Albright. This is my mom's shop. Are you looking for anything special?"

"Um, just browsing," I tell her. Really, I'm looking for a clue that might tell me where I am and what's going on, but I can't exactly say that, or she'll think, just like the kids at my new school, that I'm a weirdo.

"Hey," she says, pointing at the rainbow ribbon in my hair. "I have a ribbon just like that! I used to have two, but I lost one."

I'm about to ask her whether it might be in her window seat when the song on the radio fades and the deejay cuts in. "That was a brand-new tune by KC and the Sunshine Band. Stay tuned if you're groovin' for this week's number one hit by Barry Manilow." Wait—a new tune by an oldies disco group? I suppose it could be. But Barry Manilow—wasn't he popular like a million years ago?

Then I notice the calendar pinned to the wall. *September,* it says . . . *1975.*

❀ *Turn to page 16.*

ave I traveled back in time? I look down at the mood ring in amazement. It didn't take me to a different place, but to a different *time*.

While I'm puzzling on this, Julie interrupts my thoughts. "Hey, I like your mood ring! I have one just like it, somewhere up in my room."

Her room? Of course, it's all making sense now—if it's possible for time travel to make any sense. My room was *her* room in 1975. So, could this be Julie's mood ring from the 1970s? I swallow hard. "Look, it's gray," I say, trying to keep my hand from shaking as I show her the ring. "Can you tell me what that means?"

"Hmm," she says, raising an eyebrow. "Gray means you're nervous."

I bite my lip. Nervous—no surprise there. Who wouldn't be nervous about traveling back in time?

Julie tosses her ball into the air. "Do you play basketball?"

In spite of my confusion, my face lights up. "I love basketball!"

Julie smiles. "We could head to the park and shoot some hoops when you're done shopping."

Chloe and I used to love playing HORSE in her

driveway back in Ohio. "Sure, that would be fun," I tell Julie. Making friends is easy in 1975! So why is it so hard in the twenty-first century?

Julie shows me around the store, pointing out the apple-seed bracelets that are really popular among her classmates, and the fuzzy foot-shaped rugs just like the one she has in her room. I buy a flower-power necklace charm with the Kennedy half-dollar in my pocket and get a 1966 quarter back, which is not as cool as the half-dollar, but still, it's almost fifty years old in my time!

As Julie and I start to head out the door, her mom calls out, "Oh, Julie? Don't forget that your dad is coming to pick you up tonight at five o'clock."

"Right," Julie says. Then she winces. "Is Tracy coming this time?"

Her mom shrugs. "You know your sister."

Julie gives a heavy sigh and shoves the door open. I follow her outside and notice that her mood has darkened.

"You okay?" I ask her.

She shrugs. "Let's just say that if I had that mood ring on right now, it would be amber. Anxious

amber." She bounces her basketball against the wall. "The truth is, I just don't understand my sister, Tracy. I know teenagers can be moody and all, but we only get to see our dad on weekends now that my parents are . . . divorced." She says the *D* word in almost a whisper. "Tracy refused to see him last weekend, and now it looks like she might not come *again* this weekend." She bounces the ball to me.

I'm not sure what to say. I mean, I can hardly even talk to my own brother about these things.

Julie whips her hair around as if to shake her sister out of her mind. Suddenly she walks up to a newspaper displayed in a self-serve kiosk on the sidewalk. I read the headline over her shoulder: LITTERED BEACH MAY BE CLOSED. The black-and-white photo shows a couple of sunbathing teenagers surrounded by pop cans and trash.

Julie throws up her hands. "And now my favorite beach might close!" She turns to me with a look of helplessness. "Do you ever feel like things are just spinning out of control?"

"Boy, do I," I tell her.

Is it possible there's a reason I arrived in Julie's life

at this exact moment in history? I might not be able to help my brother, but maybe I can help my new friend. My first thought is to get her mind off her troubles by showing her the funny puppy video my dad e-mailed me yesterday—but does the Internet even *exist* in 1975? Julie likes basketball, so a game of HORSE would probably cheer her up. But what if I could help her find a way to *do* something about the things that are troubling her?

❀ *To suggest a visit to the beach,
turn to page 22.*

❀ *To find another way to distract her
from her worries, turn to page 25.*

can't let Julie down now. And I can't let this Stinger kid keep on believing that boys are better than girls. Squaring my shoulders, I look Stinger straight in the eye. "I'm in."

"Far out!" Julie says. "Game on!"

Just as we're about to start, a teenage boy and girl walk past the basketball court swinging their tennis rackets. I recognize the blonde girl from the photo in Julie's room—it must be Julie's sister, Tracy.

"Hey, Mike!" Stinger calls out to Tracy's friend. "If you guys are done playing tennis, do you want to get in on a basketball game?"

The teenagers turn to each other and grin. "Why not?" Mike says, ruffling Stinger's hair. "I'm always up for a game against my little brother."

"Actually, it's a battle of the sexes," Julie says. "So Mike's on the boys' team and Tracy's with us girls."

"Cool!" says Tracy. "It'll be like Billie Jean King's match against Bobby Riggs."

"Who are they?" I ask.

Everybody looks at me like I'm nuts.

"Where've you been?" Tracy asks. "You never heard of the big Battle of the Sexes tennis match?

Bobby Riggs said that he could beat any woman on the court and challenged tennis pro Billie Jean King to a match."

Julie adds, "But she beat him by a long shot and proved to everybody that women athletes should be taken seriously." She looks pointedly at Stinger.

"That's different," says Stinger. "This isn't tennis. This is *basketball*."

"Careful, little brother," says Mike. "I'd like to see *you* try to beat Tracy at tennis."

Stinger waves him off. "Come on. Let's just win this thing already."

Before we get started, Tracy goes over some ground rules. "We'll play to thirty-five points. No double dribbling, no holding back other players, and if you step out-of-bounds, you need to step inbounds again before you touch the ball."

"What about fouls?" I ask. "We don't have a referee. Who's going to call the fouls?"

T. J. steps in. "Let's agree that you can only call a foul if other people see the foul happen. Now, let's play!"

❀ *Turn to page 28.*

I have no idea how to help Julie with her family worries—I've got enough of those problems myself. I squat down to take a closer look at the newspaper article about the beach, and I can't help feeling disappointed. Ever since we arrived in San Francisco, I've been dying to go to the beach. I've never been to the ocean before—and Lake Erie definitely doesn't count. *If the beach closes now,* I wonder, *will it ever reopen? If I visit in the twenty-first century, will it be cleaned up? Or is it just another parking lot now?*

"Maybe it's not as bad as they say," I tell Julie, trying to sound optimistic. "It can't be *that* difficult to pick up some paper cups and plastic bags off the beach."

"I dunno. Looks pretty bad to me," Julie replies.

I stand up. "Well, there's only one way to find out."

Julie looks doubtful. "Hold on. Are you suggesting we should go to the beach and start cleaning it up ourselves?"

"You bet I am!" I say.

Julie frowns, thinking, and then brightens. "Okay. Let's do it!"

We dash back into Gladrags to gather supplies.
Julie's mom watches us as we scrounge around the
utility room at the back of the store, gathering garbage
bags and rubber gloves.

"What's gotten into you two?" she asks.

"We're headed to Ocean Beach to pick up litter,"
Julie explains.

Mrs. Albright looks impressed. "What a great
idea." She gets a twinkle in her eye. "Now, if I could
just get Julie to clean up her room . . ."

I laugh and tell her my mom says the same thing
about me.

"Mom, where's Tracy?" Julie asks. "Maybe she'll
come with us. We could definitely use some help." I can
see the hope in Julie's eyes. Maybe she thinks she can
convince Tracy to go to their dad's tonight, too.

"She left early this morning to go to tennis practice,"
Mrs. Albright says. "She said she'd be at the library all
day working on a community service project with a
friend."

Julie's shoulders slump. Her mom gives her a
sympathetic shoulder squeeze and pops open the
drawer on the cash register. "Here's some money

for the shuttle bus. If you walk, you'll never get back in time for Dad to pick you up at five o'clock. Don't be late!"

❀ *Turn to page 30.*

watch Julie roll her basketball back and forth in her hands.

"Think fast!" I say as I tap the basketball out of Julie's hands and dribble it just out of her reach, daring her to steal it from me.

"Hey!" she says with a feigned scowl, but the gleam in her eyes tells me she's up for the challenge.

Our keep-away game continues as we laugh and dribble our way down the street to a nearby park. Suddenly Julie stops and calls to a bushy-haired man at the far end of the block. "Hey, Hank!" The man stops and waves. Julie grabs the ball and dribbles at a run down the sidewalk to catch up with him, and I trot behind her, trying to steal the ball.

But Hank gets there first, palming the ball and then holding it up out of Julie's reach, spinning it on one finger. "Hey, Julie, what's the news? Did you turn in that petition?"

Julie nods. "The school principal is taking a look at it. He said he should have an answer to me by next week. Keep your fingers crossed!"

Hank crosses his fingers on the hand holding the ball, and the spinning ball drops to the sidewalk. Julie

grabs it and dribbles between her legs.

Hank grins. "I'd put you on the team for sure. Catch ya later. Good luck!" As the light changes, he waves and heads across the street.

"Who's Hank, and what's this petition he was talking about?" I ask Julie as we turn the corner and continue toward the park.

"Hank was Mom's very first customer at Gladrags. He gave me the idea to do a petition to play on the basketball team."

I'm confused. "A petition to play on the basketball team? Can't anybody just join or try out?"

"If only it were that easy," she says with a sigh. "But my school only has one basketball team, and the coach says that girls aren't even allowed to try out. I asked the principal whether we could start a girls' team, but he told me the school can't afford another set of uniforms and equipment to start one."

"That's not fair," I point out.

Julie shrugs. "That's what I said in my petition. And I found an article in the newspaper about this new law called Title Nine, which says that girls deserve the same opportunities as boys in school—and that

includes playing on sports teams. There are still a lot of people who don't agree with the law—like Coach Manley. But there are a lot of people who do, and I got one hundred and fifty people to sign my petition. Still, the big question is whether the school principal will go along with the coach, or will agree with my petition." She sighs. "I know it's a long shot, but Hank persuaded me that I should fight for what I believe in instead of just giving up."

I'm so surprised I can't speak. I can't believe how much trouble Julie has to go through just to be able to play on a sports team! At my school, if I want to play basketball—or baseball, or even football—all I have to do is sign up.

"I sure hope you'll get a chance to play," I tell her.

"Thanks," she says, twisting her braid nervously. "Me too."

❀ *Turn to page 34.*

old on a minute," Stinger says. "I think we need some sort of prize for when the boys beat the girls."

Tracy rolls her eyes at him. "This is just a pickup game, Stinger. For fun. There's no trophy."

"Wait, I like Stinger's idea," says Julie. "If we win, we get to choose something for you boys to do for us. If you win, we have to do something for you."

The boys form their own huddle while Julie, Tracy, and I step off the court to come up with a challenge for the boys.

Julie smiles mischievously. "If we win, let's make the boys do something embarrassing in public."

"Like what?" I ask.

Tracy scans the park and her eyes land on a group of high school girls with pom-poms practicing cheers on the grass nearby. She bobs her head in their direction, and we start giggling.

When we return to the court, the boys look confident. Stinger tells us that if the boys win, we have to pack up a picnic lunch and serve it to them. "And none of that peanut butter and jelly goop," Stinger adds. "I want to see submarine sandwiches!"

"Okay," says Julie, still trying to hold back a giggle. "If we win, you guys have to go out into the center of the park and do a girl-power cheer. With pom-poms." The boys look totally shocked. Julie and I break into a goofy cheer, kicking our feet and waving our arms in the air.

"No way, no how," says Stinger. "That is so pathetic." He's starting to turn red just *thinking* about having to cheer in public.

"What do you have to worry about?" I ask Stinger. "You guys are going to beat us anyway, right?"

Stinger gives me a condescending look before joining the boys in a huddle. They whisper for a while and then clap to break the huddle.

"It's a deal," Mike says. We all shake on it.

✿ *Turn to page 36.*

ulie thanks her mom for the money, and we head out the door to catch the shuttle a few blocks away. As the bus winds through the streets, there's so much to see that I can hardly take it all in. A gigantic rainbow-colored peace sign is chalked on a brick wall. Girls in long dresses are dancing to a song on a radio. I lean near the open window to hear the song—it's Elton John! I think about my dad, who loves oldies, and try to figure out how old he was in 1975, and realize he was just a kid, like me. For him, they're not oldies—they're songs he grew up with.

When we arrive at Ocean Beach, Julie and I hop off the shuttle and cross the street to the beach entrance. The beach is much bigger than it seemed in the newspaper picture. Cups, wrappers, bags, newspapers, and all sorts of litter lie scattered across the sand, blowing around in the wind.

I take in a deep breath. Maybe it was a mistake to bring Julie here. The litter problem seems much bigger than anything just the two of us can solve. "It's worse than I thought," I say quietly.

Julie nods slowly. "We could pick up garbage for a week and it wouldn't make a difference." She pauses,

and then pulls out the garbage bags and hands one to me. "But we're here, so we might as well get started. We'll just do the best we can," Julie says, stepping into the sand. She flaps her garbage bag open and pulls on her rubber gloves.

I take my first steps onto the beach and feel a rush of excitement. The Pacific Ocean is so close, I can almost taste the salt water! I start taking my gym shoes off.

"Better keep 'em on," Julie suggests. "Look at all the bottles lying around—there may be broken glass in the sand."

I'm disappointed that I won't get to feel the Pacific Ocean sand between my toes, but she's right—it's not worth the risk.

We get started plucking litter out of the sand and tossing it into our trash bags. We haven't been working long when two park rangers approach us.

"Hi," says one. "I'm Kimberly, and this is Chip."

"Did you come to help clean up the beach?" Chip asks us, looking at our bags.

"Yeah," Julie tells them. "We saw the picture in the paper and felt like we had to do something."

Kimberly nods. "That article really called attention to the litter problem at this beach." She sweeps her arm out before us. "You're not the only ones who were inspired to show up and pitch in."

For the first time, I notice other people farther down the beach, similarly armed with trash bags. "They're all picking up litter, too?"

"That's right," Chip says. "We decided to get people organized so that we can make this as efficient as possible. Try to keep cans and bottles separate for recycling. If your bag fills up or gets too heavy, just haul it over there to the parking lot." He points to two green pickup trucks parked near the beach entrance.

"Chip and I will load the bags into the pickups and take them to a recycling center," says Kimberly. "Pretty groovy, huh?"

"Keep up the good work," Chip says. "And thank you!"

Now that we know there are others helping clean up the beach, we don't feel quite so discouraged. There's a lot to clean up, but the task no longer seems impossible.

However, after picking up the last piece of garbage

from a spit of rocks at one end of the beach, we look down into a small cove on the other side of the spit and see a ton of garbage trapped against the rocks at low tide. Julie gives me a look that says *Yikes*. We definitely have our work cut out for us.

❀ *Turn to page 41.*

Before long we arrive at the basketball court.
Two boys around our age are scrimmaging.
When the boy with shaggy hair makes a basket,
Julie lets out a whoop. "Go, T. J.!" He looks up and
brushes his hair out of his eyes before giving Julie
a thumbs-up.

The other boy narrows his eyes. "Well, if it isn't the
tomboy."

"Lay off her, Stinger," T. J. says.

Stinger dribbles his ball in a circle around Julie
and me. "Albright here thinks she's Basketball Jones,"
he says. "You don't *actually* think Coach Manley's
going to let you be a Jaguar, do you?"

"He'll have to if Principal Sanchez says so," Julie
replies coolly. Then she tosses her ball over his head,
sending it straight through the hoop.

"Lucky shot," Stinger sneers. "No way you can
play against a whole team of boys. Admit it: Boys are
just better—at sports, at everything!"

"You don't *seriously* believe that, do you?" I ask.
"Julie could beat you any day."

Stinger pastes on a cocky smile. "Oh yeah? Prove it."

"You're on," Julie says. "You and T. J. against us

girls. A battle of the sexes."

Wait . . . what? I didn't sign up for this. I was just trying to stand up for my new friend. Julie has a lot to prove, and I don't want to let her down. I've never played on a team without Chloe and my other friends, and I'm not sure I'll be any good. I don't want to be the reason Julie loses in front of this kid Stinger.

Julie looks at me and senses my hesitation. "Are you in?" she whispers.

> ❀ *To join Julie in a two-on-two game against the boys, turn to page 20.*
>
> ❀ *To find a way to stay off Julie's team, turn to page 38.*
>
> ❀ *To try to avoid playing altogether, turn to page 62.*

We flip a coin to see who will start the game.

The girls win the coin toss. Julie inbounds the ball to me. I drive downcourt and do an easy pass to Tracy, who shoots for two points! The boys take it out and drive back up the court. Mike snaps off a quick corner shot. Two points for the boys. The game goes back and forth at a steady pace. Much to the boys' surprise, we are quite evenly matched.

Stinger sticks to me like glue, and I have trouble getting around him. "Out of my way, Ponytail," he snarls, even though he's the one crowding me. He snags a pass from Mike and manages to twist out of my reach. He jumps, and I leap up to try to block his shot. But he fakes and whips the ball at me, super hard. *Ouch!* It stings off my leg and bounces out-of-bounds.

"Foul!" I shout, rubbing my leg where it still smarts.

"Boo-hoo-hoo," Stinger taunts. "What's wrong? Can't take it 'cause you're a *girl*?"

"You totally did that on purpose!"

He looks at me like I'm nuts. "What do you mean? I was just passing the ball to T. J. Can I help it if your leg got in the way?"

"Enough of that, Stinger," Tracy breaks in. "T. J. was nowhere near you when you flung that ball. She gets the foul."

As I set up for my two shots at the free-throw line, I'm feeling pleased that I caught Stinger playing dirty. But when I hear Julie and Tracy cheering for me, I'm suddenly very nervous. My nerves get the best of me, and my first shot bounces off the rim.

"You've got this," Julie calls to me.

On the second shot, the ball hits the backboard, circles the rim, and falls through the net.

Julie runs over and claps me on the back. "Way to go!"

The score is now 18–16 in favor of the boys, which means the game is more than halfway over. A small crowd has started to gather on the benches around the court, watching and cheering us all on. This has turned into a serious game—and now that we have an audience, the pressure's on.

❀ *Turn to page 46.*

I can see how important this is to Julie, and I don't want to hold her back from playing, but there's no way she'll win a game against the boys with me on her team, no matter how good she is at basketball. There's *got* to be some other way to help Julie show off her chops.

"Hey, Julie, Stinger—let's play HORSE instead!" I suggest. This way, I tell myself, Julie can still show her skills with the ball, but she won't be relying on *me* to help her win.

"I love playing HORSE!" Julie says.

The boys seem satisfied with this challenge, and Stinger tells Julie to take the first shot. "She can use all the chances she can get," he says to T. J., snickering.

Julie steps up to the free-throw line and bounces the ball a few times. Focusing on the basket, she jumps up, releasing the ball in an arc. *Swish!*

As the ball goes in, cheers erupt from the other side of the court. Julie grins and waves at two teenagers, a boy and a girl, who are watching from the sidelines and holding tennis rackets.

"That's my sister, Tracy," Julie tells me. "And that's Mike, Stinger's brother."

As Stinger steps up to the free-throw line, Mike calls over, "Hey, Stinger, you're not gonna let a girl beat you, are you?"

Tracy punches him in the arm. "Don't forget that's my little sister you're talking about, Mike."

With his big brother watching, Stinger looks more determined than ever. He bounces the ball, he jumps, and the ball grazes through the hoop.

Stinger gives his brother a thumbs-up and then turns to Julie. "Couldn't come up with a harder shot, Albright? I thought you wanted to win this thing."

Julie presses her lips together in a thin line but doesn't take the bait.

It's my turn. I'm not very good at free throws—especially in front of an audience. My feet feel like they're made of concrete. I jump up for the shot, and the ball hits the rim. I'm disappointed, but I'm relieved that I decided not to play on a team with Julie.

Julie tells me, "Don't worry. You'll make the next one." We watch T. J. go for the free throw and miss. Now T. J. and I both have an *H*.

It's Stinger's turn to pick the shot. "Go for the Statue of Liberty!" Mike calls. Stinger takes two big

steps back from the free-throw line. He holds both hands over his head and lets the ball fly with a nice backspin. It arches and goes right through the net.

I've never even heard of that shot, but I'm not about to let on. Julie makes the shot, and I'm impressed. So does T. J.

I take a deep breath and raise my arms above my head, trying to imitate the others. I count *one, two, three* and let the ball go. It doesn't go near the net.

❀ *Turn to page 49.*

As we climb down to get started, we notice a teenage boy and girl sunbathing on the far side of the cove. Julie squints. "Tracy?" she says under her breath, and then turns to me. "I think that's my sister. It looks like her hat and swimsuit. Come on, let's get a little closer."

We work our way along the waterline to the other edge of the cove. When we are near, the girl-who-might-be-Tracy sits up on her beach blanket and looks right at my new friend. "Julie?" the girl calls.

I follow Julie over. Next to their beach blanket lie two tennis rackets and a cooler, along with a portable radio that is blasting some vaguely familiar disco song. Julie eyes the boy sunbathing next to Tracy and then politely introduces me to her sister. "And that's Mike," she says, gesturing toward Tracy's friend. She gives her sister a quizzical look. "Mom said you were going to be at the library after tennis practice. Aren't you supposed to be working on a community service project with your . . . friend?"

Tracy rolls her eyes. "Get real. No one could spend a beautiful day like today inside a dingy old library."

When Julie puts her hands on her hips and looks

to her sister for an explanation, Tracy's expression softens. "Come on, Julie. Promise you won't tell? It'd really help me out if you didn't say anything to Mom."

I can see Julie struggle. She is obviously bothered that Tracy wants her to cover for her lie. Finally Julie reaches in her pocket, pulls out a plastic bag, and hands it to Tracy. "Then at least help us with the beach cleanup, since you're just lying here doing nothing."

"Doing nothing? I'm working on my tan." Tracy peers at Julie over her sunglasses and points down the beach. "Look. There are plenty of people helping already. You don't need us."

Mike takes the last sip from a bottle of Orange Crush and tosses it into Julie's garbage bag. "There. I just helped."

"Oh brother," Julie mumbles, letting out a sigh. She tugs on my sleeve and says, "Never mind. Forget them. Let's get back to work."

Julie and I continue picking up the litter strewn throughout the cove. Every once in a while, Julie glances over at her sister, but whatever's bothering her just seems to drive her to work harder.

Soon our bags of trash are filled to bulging. Julie

and I tie them up and start lugging them across the
sand. Julie stops at a spot near Tracy and Mike and—
thud—heaves the bag onto the sand dramatically, to
get her sister's attention.

"Gross! Get that garbage away from us," Tracy
says, backing up on her blanket like a sand crab.

"The whole beach is full of garbage," I remind her.
"There's no getting away from it." I point to a plastic
foam cup sticking out of the sand next to the beach
blanket.

Tracy looks at Mike. "Ugh, they're just going to
keep bothering us. Let's go," she says. They get up
and shake the sand off their blanket. The wind whips
it back in our faces, stinging our eyes.

Julie snaps, "Hey, keep your sand to yourselves!"

"Don't worry," Tracy says. "We're out of here."

Mike gives Tracy a knowing nudge, then mumbles
something and smirks.

Tracy covers a giggle with her hand. "Oh yeah,"
she says, holding out her hand to us. "Tell you what.
Since we're leaving, why don't we turn in those bags
for you?"

Julie and I glance sideways at each other, surprised

and a little confused. "Um, okay, that would be great," Julie says. "Just take them over to the green trucks at the parking lot. But what's so funny?"

"Oh, nothing. Private joke," Tracy tells her. "Remember, Julie, we were at the library all day, right?"

Before Julie can answer, Tracy and Mike sling their belongings over their shoulders and head off toward the parking lot, dragging our garbage bags behind them through the sand.

"I wonder what those two are up to," Julie says.

"Well, at least now we have more time to keep cleaning," I tell her, trying to look on the bright side.

Julie nods halfheartedly and shakes open two more big garbage bags. As we continue along the cove to finish clearing the litter, I can tell that Julie's inter-action with Tracy is still bothering her.

I'm at a loss about what to do. I suggested we come to the beach so that Julie could feel like she was fix-ing at least one thing that was wrong in her life, and it seemed like we were getting somewhere. I have a feeling she wants to face the problem with her sister head-on—just as we are doing by cleaning up the

beach—and confront Tracy about her feelings. But I know I'm not very good at confrontation—or at talking about family problems. Just the idea of seeing Julie do it makes me squirm.

❀ *To keep quiet and continue the cleanup, turn to page 53.*

❀ *To help Julie find her sister, turn to page 64.*

We change our strategy to man-to-man. I volunteer to cover Stinger, determined to keep an eye on him and guard him close. I'm staying tight on Stinger when I notice that his shoelace is untied and dragging on the ground behind him. I know I shouldn't, but it's just too tempting—I step on it and keep my shoe planted in that spot. When he pivots to grab a pass from T. J., he trips and falls—*splat*—flat on the ground. I can't help giggling as he struggles to get up.

He jumps up and spits out, "Foul! You did that on purpose."

T. J. points to Stinger's untied lace. "I think *that's* what tripped you. Tie your shoe and let it go, man."

My face burns with Stinger's glare on me. I look the other way, feeling a twinge of guilt but also relieved that nobody saw what I did.

The game picks up, and we're drenched in sweat. Both teams score several more points, and Stinger seems to be getting more frustrated with every basket the girls' team scores. He seems more focused on keeping me away from the ball than on scoring points for his own team.

"Wake up, Stinger," Mike calls to him when a way-

ward pass from Julie zings past him. I grab the ball and send it into the basket. The girls are in the lead! Tracy makes another basket, and we're feeling confident. But the boys fight back, and before we know it, the score is 34–33.

Game point, and the boys are ahead by just one point. Whoever scores next wins the game *and* the Battle of the Sexes. From across the court, Julie's eyes meet mine and she gives me a huge smile. I feel a rush of excitement. We've got this game locked up!

The boys have the ball, and T. J. is driving down to half-court. Julie glides past him, cleanly stealing the ball. She dribbles for the basket, but can't get close. I'm wide-open, and she passes it to me. If I can just make my signature Hula Hoop shot . . .

Out of nowhere, Stinger charges at me. Just as I'm starting into my jump to make the shot, I feel a tug from behind. The ball spills out of my hands and rolls out-of-bounds as I land with a *thunk*. When I look up, Stinger's right there, grinning wildly.

I look around the court. *Didn't anybody see what he did?* That sneaky Stinger came up from behind and pulled my shirt to keep me from making the shot!

I run my fingers along the back of my shirt and feel where the fabric has been stretched out. Even though nobody saw what Stinger did, he won't be able to deny it once I show them the evidence. So I *could* call the foul—and if I make both free throws, we'll win the game.

But then I think about when Stinger called the foul on me. I deserved the foul, and if he had made even one of those free-throw shots, then the boys would be celebrating a win right now. Plus, everybody thought Stinger was being a sore loser when he called the foul on me, because nobody knew I had stepped on his shoelace on purpose. I've already called one foul on Stinger—won't I just look like a sore loser for calling another?

❀ *To call a foul, turn to page 51.*

❀ *To keep quiet, turn to page 95.*

ir ball!" Stinger calls out. "Hey, Albright, your sidekick's as rusty as the Tin Man."

"At least *she* has a heart!" Julie retorts.

I'm fuming inside, but I stay quiet as I decide the shot for the next round. I dribble straight down the middle of the court, and when I'm almost under the hoop, I spin around and do a fadeaway, jumping away from the net and releasing the ball at the top of my jump. *Swish!*

"Wow!" Julie says. "Where'd you learn that shot?

I blush. "My dad taught it to me. My best friend Chloe calls me Hula Hoop whenever I do it."

Julie giggles. "Hula Hoop. That's a good one."

Julie tries to make my Hula Hoop shot, but she spins too far and throws an air ball that goes up and over the backboard. She laughs at herself as she goes after the ball, realizing how funny she looked. T. J. is laughing so much that his shot doesn't even make the backboard.

Stinger is smirking, too, but turns serious as he takes a running start. However, he trips over his own feet and nearly falls on his face. Now he has an *H*, just like Julie and T. J.

Proud that my Hula Hoop shot cost Stinger a letter,

I feel my confidence coming back. I make the next several shots in a row. Tracy and Mike continue to cheer us on in the background. T. J. spells HORSE first and is out of the game. After the next round, I'm out, too, but I don't mind because Julie still has a chance to win. It's down to her and Stinger, who both have just one letter left.

❀ *Turn to page 56.*

Foul!" I call out, deciding to risk it. I hold out my shirt, showing the others where it's all stretched out from Stinger grabbing it.

Stinger throws his hands in the air defensively and shouts, "No way. I never touched your stupid shirt."

"I didn't see what happened," T. J. says with a shrug.

Mike hesitates, looks his brother in the eye, and gives him a chance to tell the truth.

Stinger glares at me. I can tell that he's trying to figure out a way to call me out for stepping on his shoelace, but he knows he doesn't have any proof.

Mike won't wait any longer. He sighs and bounces the ball to me. "Looks like you get your free throws."

Here I am again at the free-throw line. A pin-drop hush falls over the crowd, and I can practically hear my own heart thumping in my chest. I plant my feet in place, dribble three times, raise the ball behind my head, and . . .

Swish! I make the basket. Julie and Tracy go crazy, jumping around me and screaming. Stinger kicks the ground. The game is tied 34–34. I still have to make the second shot if we're going to win the game.

Before she steps back to her spot next to Tracy, Julie gives me a hug. "Thank you," she whispers. "Whether or not we win today, I'm so glad you were on my team."

"Me too," I whisper. But at that same moment, I realize that Julie doesn't care about winning at all costs—she cares about being a team and winning by *skill*, not tricks. It's true that Stinger didn't play fair, but neither did I.

All eyes are on me now. Suddenly I'm not sure I want to make this basket, but I have to at least try. I push the prickle of guilt to the back of my mind and block out the shouting crowd. As the ball releases from the tips of my fingers, it seems to go in slow motion. I feel disappointment—and then relief—when the ball boings off the rim.

❀ *Turn to page 57.*

I decide that the best way to help Julie feel better is to bring her attention back to the beach cleanup. The litter is a problem I know we can help solve—while Julie's problems with Tracy seem much bigger and deeper than anything I can help fix.

"How about we make this fun and turn the cleanup into a treasure hunt?" I suggest to Julie. "Let's see who can find the coolest treasure!"

Julie perks up at my suggestion, and her energy seems renewed as we sift through the garbage we find along the edge of the cove. In between picking up pop-tops, cigarette butts, and fishing bobbins, we find some smooth pebbles, a crab claw, and a few pieces of polished beach glass. Julie picks up a periwinkle, and I find a piece of rainbow-colored shimmery abalone shell that I tuck into my pocket for safekeeping.

After about a half hour, as we're fishing out the last pieces of debris to put into our nearly full bags, I hear a squeak. Or at least I think I do.

"Did you hear that?" I ask Julie.

"Hear what?" Silence. She turns back to her garbage bag and ties it closed.

Dropping my trash bag, I clamber up onto a rock.

From up here, I can see the entire beach. The water sparkles in the sun, like the blue-green color of my mood ring. I close my eyes and listen hard, but all I hear is the lapping of the waves. It must have been a distant seagull, I decide.

"You coming?" Julie says, holding her bag up to signal that she's ready to go turn it in.

"Yeah," I tell her, and return to my garbage bag.

Then I hear the noise again. I put my finger to my lips, signaling for Julie to stop and listen. We wait, pricking up our ears.

Eee! Eee! It sounds like a cry or a whimper.

We look around in every direction. "I think it's coming from over there," Julie says, pointing. "From those rocks at the edge of the water."

We run in that direction, and sure enough, the crying sound gets louder. Julie starts to work her way across the rocks, but I hesitate. The wind has picked up, and waves are crashing closer to the shore.

"What if the tide comes in and we can't get back?" I ask.

"But what if somebody's in trouble? We have to go see if we can help."

I look to the nearest beach patrol house and see a woman sitting inside, scanning the beach with a pair of binoculars.

I turn to follow Julie over the barnacled rocks. "Be careful!" I call, scraping my knees as I go.

We search around frantically, studying the crevices between the rocks. *Eee! Eee!* The sound is right under my nose. Squatting down, I can see a jumble of kelp wedged into the space between two rocks. I use a stick to pull loose some of the kelp. Then I catch a glimpse of wet fur between the pulpy leaves.

❀ *Turn to page 70.*

Stinger chooses the shot. He walks up to the free-throw line. *Wait, didn't he make fun of Julie for picking such an "easy" shot?* With a sly smirk, he turns his back toward the hoop, dips the ball between his legs, and sends the ball over and behind his head. Ugh—he makes the basket. Julie bites her lip and steps forward to take her turn.

"Go, Julie!" I yell from the sidelines.

She lobs the ball over her head and closes her eyes. *Boing!* The ball bounces off the rim.

Stinger pumps both fists in the air. "H-O-R-S-E! You're a horse! I win! You should stick to the girly stuff, Albright. Why don't you go paint your nails or something?"

"Give it a rest, Stinger," T. J. says. "It was a good game."

But Stinger has to take it one step further. He nudges T. J. and says, "I told you that girls weren't meant to be Jaguars."

Julie's shoulders slump. I run after her as she shuffles off the court.

❀ *Turn to page 68.*

ulie and Stinger dive for the ball when it bounces between them. The rest of us are frozen, watching the battle. Julie snatches the ball a split second sooner, but Stinger knocks it free. They dive for it again, hands and elbows flying. Stinger almost has control when Julie slides low, scooping the ball right out of his grasp. She spins, drives, jumps up for a layup . . . and scores a hard-fought two points.

"Girls win!" I yell.

Julie and I jump up and down in a bear hug as the crowd cheers.

"Hey, good game," Mike says, clapping Julie on the back. We shake hands all around.

"C'mon, admit it, Stinger," T. J. says. "The girls beat us fair and square."

"Yeah we did!" Tracy says, pumping her fist in the air.

"I guess," Stinger says, looking at the hoop like he can't believe what just happened. I can't help beaming at Julie. The win is even sweeter now that we won because of her super-quick moves.

Mike bounces the ball as he walks toward his gym bag on the sidelines. Stinger and T. J. follow.

"Not so fast!" Julie and I call out to the boys.

Tracy says, "Aren't you guys forgetting something? A little bet we made?"

T. J. gulps. Mike hits his forehead. Stinger says, "Let's run for it!" and Mike has to pull him back by his shirt.

"A bet's a bet, guys," Mike admits. "We all shook on it."

Stinger looks stunned. "Pom-poms? Are you cracked? You mean we're really gonna shake *pom-poms*?"

Julie and I run to the girls in the park who were practicing cheers. We explain to them about our Battle of the Sexes basketball game and our bet with the boys.

"Do you think we could borrow your pom-poms for a few minutes?" Julie asks.

"Only if we get to come watch!" one of the girls giggles.

Julie grins. "The more the merrier."

We drag the boys to the center green, next to the playground and picnic area. Julie hands them the pom-poms, and the two cheerleaders show them some

moves, complete with high kicks in the air.

Julie and I gather our audience from the basketball game and invite some kids in the park to come watch.

Stinger turns three shades of red. "Like this isn't embarrassing enough!"

"Okay, guys," Mike says. "Ready?"

"Give me a G! Give me an I! Give me an R! Give me an L! Give me an S!" they shout, waving their arms and kicking their big sneakers in the air like clowns. "What does it spell? GIRLS!" The crowd cheers.

"You said it, boys!" Tracy calls. Julie and I hoot and pump our fists in the air.

"Girl power!" Mike trills, hamming it up. T. J. is now doubled over with laughter, and even Stinger is grinning sheepishly, as if he finally sees the humor in it. T. J. tries to turn a cartwheel, but he falls on his backside in the grass. The crowd roars with laughter. When the boys finish, everybody cheers.

Tracy teases Mike, "You're good, you know. You really should try out for head cheerleader at the high school."

The two cheerleaders plead, "No way! Just go back to playing basketball. Leave the cheers to us. Please!"

We all laugh. As the boys turn to go, Stinger calls over his shoulder, "See you on the courts at school!"

Julie is all smiles on the way back to Gladrags. Once we're standing in front of the store, I tell her it's time for me to go home, adding, "I sure hope you make it on the team, Julie. You're a really good player."

"Thanks," she says as we share a good-bye hug. "And thanks for being such a good teammate today."

I whisper in her ear, "If you can convince Stinger, you can convince anybody."

As Julie disappears inside the shop, I realize that she has convinced *me* of something, too. I was so scared to be on a team without Chloe. But in just one game, Julie made me understand that I can make a difference on any team, even one that I just joined. When I get home, I'm going to sign up for the basketball team at my school.

I press myself against the wall of the building and make sure no one is looking before slipping off the ring. A *whoosh* and a spin later and I am standing before the storefront that used to be Gladrags. Now it's the coffee shop that sells those delicious mini

muffins and chocolate shakes that Zack likes so much.

And that's when I realize that there's more than one team that I need to be a part of. I run upstairs to get Zack.

I find him in his room, his eyes wet with tears.

I realize that even though I can't fix Mom and Dad's problems, I can still help Zack feel better about our move—and our family. For one thing, I can make sure he doesn't feel so alone anymore.

I put my arm around him, and we start to talk.

✿ *The End* ✿

To read this story another way and see how different choices lead to a different ending, turn back to page 48.

It's true that I can't stand the idea of making a fool of myself on the court—especially if it means that I might lose the game for Julie. But then it occurs to me that even if Julie and I win a game against the boys, it won't earn her a place on the basketball team.

I step between Stinger and Julie. "Julie doesn't *need* to prove herself to you or anyone else. Girls can do any-thing boys can do." I can feel my face reddening, but I keep going. "But do you know why Julie deserves to be on the team more than anybody? Because she's willing to fight for it."

"W-well, I mean . . . sh-she—" Stinger stammers.

Before he can say anything else, Julie grins at me. "Come on," she says, hooking her arm in mine. "Let's get out of here." We stride away without looking back.

"Wow, you sure let him have it," she whispers, lean-ing in close.

I bite my lip. "Was I too hard on him?"

"Gosh, no! But did you see his face?" Julie lets out a laugh. "Stinger's always so cocky—I've never seen him speechless before!"

"I hope you don't mind that I didn't want to play basketball with him," I say. "I just couldn't stand the

idea of watching that kid strut around like a peacock for much longer."

Julie giggles and starts flapping her elbows and bobbing her head.

"Your peacock looks like a chicken," I tell her, and we both crack up.

Once we pull ourselves together, Julie dribbles her basketball a couple of times. "So if we're not going to play basketball, what should we do?"

I look around the park without a clue. I don't really know where we are, and even if I did, I wouldn't know what else is nearby. "Is there anything cool around here?"

"Are you kidding me?" Julie asks. "Haven't you ever been to Golden Gate Park?"

I shake my head. "I only moved to San Francisco a week ago."

"Well, come on, then!" she says, grabbing my hand.

"Where are you taking me?" I ask with a laugh.

"You'll see!"

❀ *Turn to page 72.*

Even though the thought of confronting Tracy makes me feel uncomfortable, I realize that I need to put aside my own worries and be a good friend to Julie.

"I have an idea," I tell her. "After we finish filling up these bags and drop them off at the parking lot, let's go and find Tracy so that you can work things out with her."

"You wouldn't mind?" Julie asks. I can almost see the gears turning in her head. "I think I might know where she went with Mike. If I could just talk to her, I'd feel a little better about, well . . . everything."

"I know you would," I say. "My little brother's the same way."

We set to work filling up our bags. When we're done, we stand at the edge of the cove to admire how clean it looks now. The sand sparkles in the sun as the surf sweeps along the shore.

"Let's go up there," Julie suggests, pointing to a bluff at the edge of the cove where a few people with binoculars are standing to look out at the ocean. "It's the perfect lookout point. We can see the entire beach from there!"

We run toward the bluff, kicking up sand and feeling the wind muss our hair. I find a well-worn path that leads us up the hill and wave to Julie to follow. When we reach the bluff, Julie and I are almost breathless, looking down at the half-moon cove and the long stretch of Ocean Beach. Sandpipers scurry along the shoreline, and gulls flit and perch on the rocks below. Best of all, there's not a piece of litter in sight.

I look at Julie, and she's on tiptoe, almost lifting off the ground. She turns to me and gives me a hug. "Can you believe how pretty it looks? Thanks for coming up with such a great idea. I couldn't have done it without you."

We run back down the trail, grab our bags, and haul them to the green trucks. Julie waves to Kimberly, the ranger.

"You know what you need around here?" Julie asks. "A lot more trash cans."

I chime in. "If you had extra trash cans up and down the sidewalk, instead of just those two at the edge of the parking lot, I bet a lot more people would pick up their trash and throw it away."

Julie nods. "Maybe they would put their litter in

cans if they didn't have to walk so far out of their way."

Kimberly studies the sidewalk where we're pointing. "You know, you have a good point. I don't know why there aren't more trash cans along here. I'm going to make that suggestion when I get back to the office."

Chip, the other ranger, comes over and compliments us on collecting two whole bags that are practically bigger than we are.

"Plus two more that were brought over earlier, so that makes four," Julie says proudly.

"Really? Great! I must have missed you when you dropped off the first two bags."

"Well, actually, it was my teenage sister and her friend who dropped them off. A boy and a girl carrying tennis rackets? They turned in the first two big bags for us. Didn't you see them?" Julie asks. "It was about half an hour ago."

Kimberly wrinkles her brow, looking confused. "Yes, they were here, and they did turn in two big bags. But we thought they collected that trash themselves." She exchanges a look with Chip. "They asked us to sign a couple forms for them to verify that they had contributed to the beach cleanup for some sort of

community project assignment."

Julie looks stung, and the rangers quickly try to smooth things over. "The main thing is, you girls did a terrific job," Chip tells us, "and most important, the beach is so much cleaner now."

"Thanks," I say to the rangers. "We're super happy we could help, and besides, it was fun." I glance at Julie, but her mouth is fixed in a tight line as if she just ate an entire lemon.

Chip and Kimberly take our bags and heave them into one of the pickups.

"Let's go find your sister," I tell Julie.

She nods, her eyes filled with tears.

❀ *Turn to page 74.*

on't listen to him, Jules," Tracy calls from the sidelines. I'm hoping Tracy will come over—I think Julie would appreciate her sister's support—but she's quickly distracted by Mike showing off with Stinger's basketball. It's up to me to make Julie feel better.

"Tracy's right," I tell her. "You played a great game out there. And you came so close to winning."

"I don't care about losing some silly old HORSE game," Julie says with a wave of her hand. "But maybe Stinger's right. Maybe girls—maybe *I'm* not good enough to be a Jaguar."

I can't believe what Julie's saying. "Do you really think that you don't deserve to be on the basketball team just because you're a girl?" I ask her.

She looks at the ground and shrugs. "No, but—"

"What if Coach Manley called you tomorrow and said that you could try out? Would you give up before you had even gotten a chance to prove yourself?"

"Of course not," she says, standing up a little straighter. She narrows her eyes at Stinger, who is practicing passing drills with T. J., and marches toward him.

He sees Julie approaching and smirks. "Back for more humiliation?"

She squares her shoulders. "How about a real game? One-on-one."

"Time-out. Hold on a second," says Mike. "You guys already had your time on the court. It's our turn now." He nudges Tracy. She looks ruefully at Julie and mouths "Sorry."

Stinger dusts his hands off. "Guess you had your chance. Come on, T. J." He picks up his ball, and he and T. J. head off the court.

Since I didn't have the courage to join Julie for a real game when I had the chance before, the least I can do is help her now. "Wait!" I call to the boys. Everyone freezes and looks at me. I'm not sure what I'm asking them to wait for, but I know I have to do something.

❀ *To stand up to the teenagers,*
   turn to page 78.

❀ *To take Julie's challenge elsewhere,*
   turn to page 85.

ulie!" I call, waving her over. "I've found something!"

She scrambles over the rocks to join me.

"Do you see that?" I ask, pointing to the fur. We edge a little closer and use our gloved hands to pull away at the kelp. Soon we've exposed the creature's head.

"It's a sea otter!" Julie cries.

"It's so small—I thought they were bigger. It must be a baby," I say, as a wave comes crashing in.

The little creature squeals in the surf and blinks its dark eyes at us, as if pleading for help.

"The tide's coming in," Julie says urgently. "We have to do something—fast."

"We can't leave him," I say, as another wave crashes on the rocks. "It's going to take two of us to untangle all the kelp. Otherwise he might drown."

Then I remember the beach patrol. I jump up and wave both of my hands in the air. The woman in the patrol house perks up and starts running over.

"We found a baby sea otter, and he's in trouble," I call to her. "Please, go call animal rescue. Quickly!"

She waves and runs back to the patrol house.

Meanwhile, Julie and I set to work trying to free the little otter from the tangle of kelp.

It isn't long before we realize that the situation is worse than we thought. As I pull some strands of kelp away from the otter's midsection, I notice a clear band of plastic wrapped around its neck and another plastic band twisted around its legs.

"What is that?" I ask, and Julie shakes her head. It's too strong for us to break; it will have to be cut with a knife.

We continue clearing away the kelp and discover that the otter is tangled in plastic rings that once carried a six-pack of soda cans. What is taking the ranger so long to get here?

"He could suffocate if he starts to struggle," Julie says. "We need to cut this stuff away before . . . before it's too late."

❀ *Turn to page 116.*

We run down the sidewalk for a couple of blocks. Then Julie slows to a walk and points straight ahead. In front of us is one of the most beautiful sights I have ever seen: In the middle of a flower garden stands a magnificent white building all made out of sparkling windows. Even its great dome is made of windowpanes, like an enormous faceted diamond. It's the biggest greenhouse I've ever seen, as big as a palace.

"What is this place?" I ask Julie.

"It's the Conservatory of Flowers," Julie says. "Come on, let's go inside."

Julie and I stroll along brick paths surrounded by lush green leaves, succulents, and brightly colored blooms. In awe, we admire fiery red hibiscus flowers the size of dinner plates, bright pink ginger blossoms, and sunny yellow orchids. It's so beautiful that I wish I could bring my mother and Zack here—and suddenly I realize that I probably can. Golden Gate Park still exists, so this place is probably still here in my time, too. For the first time, I start to think it might not be so bad living here in San Francisco. I feel a pang when I think about how much Chloe would

love this place—she goes crazy for pretty flowers. Maybe she could come visit me for spring break, and I could bring her here. The tropical flowers would seem even more amazing after a snowy Ohio winter!

Julie interrupts my thoughts by pointing out some coiled green plants that look as if they could be related to some sort of chameleon.

"Fiddlehead ferns," I say, reading aloud the little nameplate below the plant. "What a funny name!"

Julie giggles. Then her eyes lock on something behind me, and her smile fades.

"Great," she says. "It's the Water Fountain Girls."

"The who?" I spin around and see three girls our age coming up the path.

"Angela, Amanda, and Alison," Julie whispers. "Triple-A meanies from my class at school."

❁ *To face the girls,*
   turn to page 80.

❁ *To avoid a confrontation,*
   go online to **beforever.com/endings**

e walk across the parking lot in silence at first, but after a few minutes Julie opens up. "I can't believe Tracy. First she lies to Mom about where she's going, and then she lies to *me* and cheats on her project. It's like I don't even know my own sister anymore."

"You said you thought you might know where she went," I prompt her.

Julie's eyes drift away, gazing up the hill toward a three-story, flat-roofed, bright blue building jutting out over the bluff. "See that big blue building? It's a restaurant called the Cliff House. They have a museum downstairs with all kinds of old-fashioned penny-arcade games and pinball machines. Tracy loves going there whenever we come to the beach. I'll bet you any money that's where she and Mike went."

At the entrance to the Cliff House museum, Julie pushes through heavy double doors that are decorated like a backgammon board. A witch-like cackling startles me as we step inside, and I look up to see a grinning, six-foot-tall automated doll staring down at me and ushering me in with a mechanical sweep of her manne-quin hand. I shudder and grab Julie's arm. Julie hardly notices; she is laser-focused on finding her sister.

As we wind through the museum, I hear the plinking of a player piano in the background and the poinging sounds of pinball machines. I realize that I'm rubbing the stone on my mood ring. I hold up my hand. The stone is gray—gray for nervous.

If *I'm* nervous about the looming confrontation, I can't imagine how Julie must be feeling.

We pass an arm-wrestling machine, a robot barber-shop quartet, and one of those claw machines full of stuffed-animal prizes. When we go by a mysterious-looking Gypsy fortune-teller machine, I have a sudden impulse to give it a try. Without letting Julie out of my sight, I stop and fish the quarter out of my pocket. I slide it into the machine and pull the lever. A small card appears in a slot down by my knees, and I grab it just as Julie slips out of view. Rushing after her through a maze of kids and parents, I glance down to read my fortune:

Danger is just around the corner.

I hurry to catch up with Julie as she's about to enter the next room. I follow on her heels, feeling an inexplicable sense of dread. I tell myself that it's just a silly

fortune, no more meaningful than something you get in a fortune cookie. But after my experience with the mood ring, I know I'm not convinced. I mean, if a mood ring can magically transport me decades into the past, then maybe a fortune-telling machine can . . . well, tell my fortune. I squeeze the ring, feeling for the stone—and that's when I notice that something terrible has happened: The stone in my ring—it's gone!

A rush of panic makes my heart race as I stare at the empty setting of my ring. One of the prongs is bent back. I take a deep breath and try to calm myself down. *Maybe the ring will still work without the stone,* I tell myself.

But if it doesn't, then—I can't even let myself finish that thought.

Just stay calm. Don't worry until you know whether the ring will work without the stone.

"I'll be right back," I yell to Julie, and hurry off to find the bathroom.

Alone in a bathroom stall, I close my eyes before twisting the ring and pulling it off my finger. There's no *whoosh*, no dizzy feeling like before. I open my eyes. I'm still in the bathroom stall.

I suddenly feel sick. This can't be happening. I won't

be able to get back to my own time if I can't find that stone, and it could be *anywhere* in the arcade.

I dash out of the bathroom and spot Julie in the next room. "Julie!" I call. "I need your help!"

Julie starts to turn to me, but then she freezes in place. I don't have to follow her gaze to know that she has spotted her sister. She glances back at me with a look that says *I need your help—please!*

I feel dizzy with all of the thoughts swirling in my head. Julie's counting on me. After all, it's because of me that she's here, getting ready to face her sister.

Can looking for the stone wait? What if I wait so long that someone finds the stone and tosses it in the garbage—or keeps it? I could really use another set of eyes to help me look for it, but it doesn't seem right to pull Julie away now that she's found Tracy, and it doesn't seem right to abandon her, either.

❁ To look for the missing stone now,
    turn to page 88.

❁ To join Julie as she confronts Tracy,
    turn to page 114.

We were here first," I tell the teenagers. I look to Julie for some backup and she jumps right in.

"Yeah," she says. "We'll play you for the court. Fourth graders versus teenagers. Whoever reaches thirty-five points first wins."

"Piece of cake," says Mike. "We could beat you munchkins with a hand tied behind our backs."

"Wait a minute," Stinger says to his brother. "No way am I playing with girls on my team."

"Either play with the girls or don't play at all," Tracy says matter-of-factly. "Your choice."

To be honest, I'm not sure I want to be playing on a team with Stinger, either. But it's worth it if it means that Julie will see she deserves a spot on the Jaguars.

Stinger huffs, but grabs the ball. The game begins.

From the first rally back and forth across the court, we can see that Mike and Tracy are strong opponents, even though it's just the two of them against the four of us. Every time I go for a pass, Tracy is there to block it. Whenever Julie or T. J. tries for a basket, Mike knocks the ball out of their hands. Then I begin to realize that these aren't the only reasons our team isn't scoring points.

The next time we have the ball, Stinger looks for T. J.,

but Tracy is all over him. "Pass to Julie!" T. J. yells, as Julie waves her arms right under the hoop. Instead, Stinger goes for the point—and misses by a long shot.

Again and again, Stinger refuses to pass the ball to Julie or me, even when we're wide-open. Mike and Tracy catch on and stick like glue to T. J. whenever Stinger has the ball.

After a bit, the score is 16–10, and the teenagers have blocked every single one of Stinger's passes to T. J. The next time Stinger ignores me and Tracy intercepts the ball before T. J. can reach it, I'm fed up.

"I was right there!" I yell to Stinger.

Stinger just ignores me. Then T. J. passes the ball to me. I'm at a strange angle and don't have a clear shot at the basket. Stinger fakes left and is standing right under the basket ready for my pass. If I go for the shot and miss, our team won't score *any* points. But if I pass to Stinger, I'll probably never get the ball back. Tracy is coming right at me—I need to decide *now*.

❀ *To pass the ball to Stinger, turn to page 91.*

❀ *To try to make a basket, turn to page 98.*

hey couldn't be as bad as that Stinger kid," I tell Julie.

Julie blows a strand of hair out of her eyes. "You'll see," she says, offering a polite nod as the girls approach.

"Hey, Tomboy," says one of the girls. She doesn't even look at me.

"Nice *sweat* shirt," another one says, holding her nose. She nudges the girl next to her. "Right, Alison?"

"Yeah," Alison says. "Is that the Jaguars uniform they gave you to hide the fact that you're a girl?"

"Yeah, right," says the first one. "Like Coach Manley is ever going to let some *girl* be on a sports team."

Julie doesn't miss a beat. "Just you wait and see, Angela," she says. "Principal Sanchez is looking over my petition right now. He might say yes."

"I won't hold my breath," Angela says. She flips her hair at Julie and walks ahead, forcing the other two to run and catch up with her.

Julie wrinkles her nose at them before turning to me. "It's no fun being the new girl," she mumbles.

I whip around. "Wait. You're a new girl, too?"

As we walk out of the conservatory, Julie explains that after her parents' divorce, she and her mom and

Tracy moved from a few miles away to live in the apartment above her mom's new store. "I just started a few weeks ago at Jack London Elementary. What school do you go to?"

I tell her, but she doesn't recognize the name. I realize that my school may not have even been built yet in Julie's time. "I miss my old school in Ohio," I tell her before she can ask any more questions. "I miss my old friends." To my surprise, tears prick in the corners of my eyes. I try to blink them away, but Julie can tell I'm upset. She guides me over to a nearby bench.

"The first few weeks are the hardest," she assures me. "That was a rough time for me, too. But then I met T. J., and things started looking up. I'm sure you'll make some friends soon."

"I'm not so sure about that," I tell her. "I've only been at my school a week, and I've already managed to make some enemies. It seems like every single person at my school is a Water Fountain Girl." I tell her about the sign that somebody put on my back. "It basically said I was a walking freak show. The worst part is, I didn't even know it was there for most of the morning. I kept wondering why everybody was

pointing and whispering behind my back."

Julie frowns. "That's awful. How did you find out that the note was there?"

"I sat in front of this girl named Savannah in social studies. She pulled the note off and handed it to me."

Julie perks up. "Well, there's some good news! It sounds like you made a friend already."

Maybe she's right, I think. Savannah *was* nice to me at school, and she's in most of my classes. Maybe on Monday I could ask to sit with her at lunch.

But then I feel a twinge of guilt. Was Chloe really worried when she asked me whether I had replaced her with a new best friend? Would she be upset with me if I found a *second*-best friend in San Francisco?

"Did you have a best friend at your old school?" I ask Julie.

Julie nods enthusiastically. "Her name is Ivy. She lives across the street from my old house—my dad's house. She's still my best friend, but I don't get to see her every day the way I used to."

I remember noticing the picture on Julie's dresser that said JULIE + IVY = BEST FRIENDS.

"When we lived across the street from each other,"

Julie continues, "we would flick our lights on and off to say good night before we went to bed." She swallows, and I can see some sadness in her eyes.

"Is it hard to stay friends after moving away?" I ask her, thinking of Chloe.

Julie considers this a moment. "Well, I still see her when I go to my dad's, and we talk on the phone a lot. But it's not the same." She pauses, as if trying to decide how much to tell me, and then says, "Now that we go to separate schools and have different lives, we don't always understand each other. A week ago we got into our first bad fight, over my basketball petition. But then we made up, when she sent me a petition to be my best friend! Now we're closer than ever, because we know that no matter what, we'll always be best friends."

I wonder what I could send Chloe to reassure her that I will always be *her* best friend.

Julie smiles and claps her hands together. "And I'll get to see her tonight when I go to my dad's for our weekend visit!"

I'm happy for Julie, but I'm suddenly feeling very homesick. I want to go home and call Chloe. I'll ask her to tell me all about the party, and I'll tell her about the

Conservatory of Flowers. And maybe tonight, I'll ask Mom if Chloe might be able to visit over spring break.

As Julie and I leave the park and head up Frederick Street, nearing the block where her—and my—apartment is, I turn to her. "I'm so glad that I met you, Julie. It's good to know that I have a friend in San Francisco."

Julie nods. "I'm here whenever you need me."

When we arrive at Gladrags, I suddenly get an idea. "Before I go, I thought of one more thing I need to buy," I tell her as we enter the store.

After I pay for my purchase, I say good-bye to Mrs. Albright and give Julie a good-bye hug. The bell above the door jingles as I leave the store. Once I'm outside, just before I slip off the mood ring, I open my palm and smile at the matching pink and orange flower-power charms in my hand: one for me, and one for my flower-loving best friend, Chloe.

Now I'm ready to go home.

❀ *The End* ❀

To read this story another way and see how different choices lead to a different ending, turn back to page 35.

look Stinger in the eye. "A superstar like Julie doesn't need some old basketball court to show what she's made of—do you, Julie?"

She lifts her chin and looks down her nose at Stinger's scowl. "No, I don't. In fact, I have a better idea . . ." She picks up her ball from the sideline. Suddenly she tosses it over the heads of T. J. and Stinger, then races ahead, grabs it, and dribbles down the sidewalk heading in the direction of Gladrags.

The boys and I tear after her. When we catch up, I ask where we're going.

"To the secret steps!" she whispers.

Secret steps? I know there are a lot of stairs in hilly San Francisco—some of them right on the sidewalk!— but I didn't know any of them were secret. We run the entire way, and after a few blocks, Julie stops and gestures toward a leafy grove. Panting, we step in and peer down a long flight of steep steps that are practically hidden in the canopy of green leaves. The view from the top is amazing. There are lush trees and flowering vines lining both sides of the steps, like a scene out of *The Secret Garden*. Tucked in among the trees are small cottages whose front yards face the steps.

"What'd you bring us here for?" Stinger asks.

"A speed dribble relay," Julie says, bouncing her basketball between her legs. "You and T. J. versus us girls. You have to bounce your ball on each step, down the stairs and back, and tag your teammate. The first team that finishes both rounds wins."

T. J. and I look uncertainly down the stairs, which seem to go on for blocks.

"Get ready to get creamed again, Albright," says Stinger as he and Julie ready themselves at the top step and grip the railings.

"On your mark . . ." I start.

"Get set . . ." says T. J.

"Go!" we both yell.

Julie and Stinger start down the stairs. Julie grabs the lead, but Stinger catches up to her at the first landing. He sneers at Julie and dribbles a little wider, giving her less room to maneuver her ball. Then he dribbles too wide, and their basketballs collide before careening down the steps. Julie and Stinger take off after them. T. J. and I are quick to follow. We watch helplessly as the balls gain speed with every bounce. They finally collide one last time, and each ball flies in a different direction.

Then we hear the *craaash!* of glass shattering and clinking upon the pavement.

❀ *Turn to page 93.*

As hard as I try, I can't get the image out of my head of some little boy finding the shiny stone on the ground and stuffing it into his pocket to keep as a souvenir. If I don't find that stone, I will literally be at a point of no return. I *have* to go find it.

I step up to Julie. "You can do this," I tell her.

"Right," she says and starts turning in her sister's direction. "Let's go."

"I—I'll be with you in a minute," I tell her. "There's something—something that I have to do first."

Julie blinks at me, and I can tell that she's trying to understand what could possibly be so important that I can't go with her.

"Go," I tell her, putting my hands on her shoulders. "I'll be right there. I just need a few minutes."

She nods before turning around and marching toward her sister.

In a flash, I'm out the door and retracing our steps through the museum. I look everywhere, feeling the ground all around the fortune-teller machine twice and checking the slot where the fortune card popped out. I search around the claw machine, the photo booth, and even the ledge where the barbershop-

quartet robots are displayed, but I don't see the stone anywhere.

I spot a museum employee handing out brochures at the information desk, and rush over.

The employee smiles at me. Her name tag says *Suzy*. "How can I help you?" she asks.

Nearly out of breath with worry, I ask her, "Has anyone turned in a small oval stone?"

"What color?"

"Well, it's—it changes color, actually. It came out of a mood ring."

"Hmm," Suzy says. "I don't think anyone's turned it in, but you can take a look through our lost and found." She bends down to rummage through a shelf beneath the desk and pulls out a box.

I dig through the box, and while there are plenty of cool things in there that my best friend Chloe would go positively gaga over—a pair of enormous round sunglasses, a paisley scarf, a smiley-face key chain—I don't see the stone from my ring.

I let out a heavy sigh and thank Suzy for her help.

"I hope you find it," she says.

I nod and try to fight back tears. I take a deep

breath and am doing my best to gather myself when
I see Julie come around the corner. She presses herself
against the wall on the other side of the room, and
a tear rolls down her cheek.

❀ *Turn to page 108.*

I spin around Tracy and swoop the ball behind my back to pass to Stinger. He catches it and quickly sends the ball into the hoop for two points.

"Good pass!" he exclaims, but when he meets my eyes he grimaces, catching himself complimenting a *girl*. "I mean, you got lucky that time."

Tracy and Mike pick up the pace and score three baskets in a row. Now our team is way behind.

Julie yells across the court, "C'mon, Stinger. I'm wide-open. Pass the ball!" But Stinger still refuses to pass the ball to either Julie or me. Finally, Julie calls a time-out.

Once we've gathered in a huddle, T. J. lets Stinger have it. "Hey, man, we're losing by a bunch. We'd have a better chance to score if you would just pass to the girls."

"Yeah," Julie agrees. "We're a team now. You can't keep hogging the ball just because you don't like having girls on the team."

Stinger rolls his eyes. "We're going to lose anyway, so what difference does it make?"

Julie's eyes narrow. "Start passing me the ball, and you'll find out!"

Despite his attitude, Stinger must have listened, because back on the court, we finally start working together as a team. Stinger passes the ball to Julie, and she goes for a basket. Score! Two points. It's a *real* game now.

After the teens get another basket, Julie passes to me. I drive down the court and do my special Hula Hoop move to spin around Mike, and—swish—another two points!

"Way to go, Hula Hoop!" T. J. shouts.

"Nice basket!" Stinger echoes, looking amazed.

❀ *Turn to page 101.*

Stinger snatches up one of the balls, which has landed in a small courtyard. Julie stands very still in front of a small red and white cottage, her eyes glued to a broken window. The other ball is gone—it must have landed inside the house.

Dogs are barking wildly from within the house. Then we hear a man's voice shout, "Who's out there?"

"Run for your life!" Stinger yells. He tucks the basketball under his arm and leaps up the stairs. T. J. bites his lip and looks at us. Without thinking, all three of us run up the stairs after Stinger.

As soon as the boys disappear over the top of the steps, we hear a door slam, and the dogs' barking gets louder. Suddenly Julie pulls me off the steps and into some bushes as we try to decide what to do. Peeking through the leaves, we see an elderly man walk out onto the steps, his dogs jumping up around him and barking. He's holding the basketball.

"Should we go back?" Julie asks.

I hesitate. *Why should we go down there alone, without Stinger and T. J.?*

"If anybody's going to take the blame, it should be Stinger," I whisper. "I saw what he did, Julie. If he

hadn't dribbled into your space, this never would have happened!"

Julie looks at me with sad eyes. "But this also wouldn't have happened if I hadn't dragged you guys over here to the secret steps."

"Still," I say, "something doesn't seem fair about surrendering without the boys. We could go down and tell the man what happened, but will he believe our story if the boys aren't here to back us up?"

"Maybe not," Julie says, her eyes lowering in disappointment. "But it also feels wrong to leave the scene of the crime. And if we go look for the boys, we might not find them."

"And even if we do find them," I add, "we might not be able to convince them to go back with us and share the blame."

❀ *To go look for Stinger and T. J.,*
turn to page 104.

❀ *To step out and take the blame,*
turn to page 110.

I decide there's no point in calling the foul.

If we're going to win, we're going to win fair and square, and I'm going to keep my pride. The play starts, and Stinger wastes no time in grabbing the ball. He inbounds to T. J. and makes a fast break for the other end of the court. T. J. sees that Mike is double-guarded at the center of the court. Meanwhile, Stinger is waving his arms, wide-open by the far basket as I fly down the court after him. T. J. throws to him, and before I can get there, Stinger makes an easy layup, and the boys have won.

They jump up and down, whooping and hollering.

I want to scream, I'm so mad at myself for not calling the foul! Stinger played dirty, and as a result, his team won. I look at Julie, expecting her to be as upset as I am. But she's smiling along with the boys and slapping them on their backs.

As we head out of the park and back to Julie's house to make submarine sandwiches for the boys, Julie notices me dragging my feet.

"You okay?" she asks.

"I think the girls should've won," I say. "I feel like it's all my fault."

Julie shakes her head. "You played a great game! We all did. And we were a good team."

"Besides," Tracy adds, "we may not have reached thirty-five points first, but we were so close."

Julie nods. "We showed them what girls can do. We'll get 'em next time."

I realize that Julie's right. What Stinger did was unfair, but it was no worse than the trick I pulled with the shoelace. And if I had called the foul and we had won on my two free throws, I would have had to live with the fact that we didn't really *earn* the win. I remind myself that the real point of the game was to show that girls are just as competitive on the court as boys—and we definitely won the day on that issue. Even Stinger can't deny that!

Back at the apartment, Julie, Tracy, and I make some awesome sub sandwiches, laughing and joking the whole time. "Let's throw in a few for us, too," says Julie.

"You two go ahead," I tell her. "But I should get going. Make an extra-large one for Stinger and tell him it's from me. A big mouth like his requires a big sandwich!"

It seems odd to go outside, knowing that the mood
ring will just take me back inside to my bedroom.
But before I slip it on, I take one last look around,
admiring the purple and turquoise house, the brightly
painted van, and the unique, fun-loving feeling of
being in San Francisco, whether in the 1970s or today.
Suddenly, I realize, this city feels like home.

❀ *The End* ❀

*To read this story another way and see how different choices
lead to a different ending, turn back to page 35.*

'mon!" Stinger urges impatiently. "I'm open!"

No way am I going to give him the satisfaction, I think to myself. I jump up to try for the two points, but Tracy is quicker—and taller—and blocks my shot.

Stinger shoots me a disgusted look. "I was right there!" he barks.

I'm just as mad, so I let him have it. "Why should I pass to you if you never pass to me?"

Julie steps in. "Come on," she says, putting her hands between us. "We're behind. If we don't do something and fast, we're going to lose to these guys."

Knowing Julie's right, I take a few deep breaths to calm down. But the next time Stinger gets the ball— and the next, and the next!— he still passes only to T. J. I'm so frustrated that I can feel the heat rising in my chest. Julie has the ball, and she tries to bounce a pass to me, but it deflects off Tracy's hand and bounces in between Stinger and me. We lock eyes and both dive for the ball. *Crash!* We slam into each other and end up in a tangle on the ground.

"Gross! Get off me," Stinger snaps.

Mike grabs the ball and runs it in for an easy two points.

"What do you two think you're doing?" T. J. yells at us as we get up and brush the dirt off our knees. "You're on the same team!"

Stinger gives me a dirty look, and I give it right back. The game continues, but it feels as if there are two different games going on: Tracy and Mike versus Julie and T. J.—and me versus Stinger.

By the time the game ends, our team has lost and I'm angrier than ever. "Thanks a lot, Stinger," I mutter to Julie. "Did you see how he was playing out there?"

Julie glances at me hesitantly, but then looks down and doesn't say a word.

T. J. breaks in. "You weren't exactly playing fair either," he says, crossing his arms. "You and Stinger were trying so hard to keep the ball away from each other that you forgot about the rest of the team."

"What? I—I mean—" I'm trying to come up with a way to explain myself, but everything I can think of doesn't sound very convincing.

Stinger interrupts my thoughts. "C'mon, man. I just wanted to win, you know? And we could've won if we didn't have to play with these girls."

"Are you from the moon?" I shout at him. "We lost

because you're a ball hog."

"Ooh, don't get your ponytail in a twist," Stinger snickers. "Girls. Always blaming somebody."

I look up at Julie, who is shaking her head. Finally, she breaks the silence. "Maybe it's true. Maybe girls and boys *can't* play together."

❀ *Turn to page 111.*

In the end, Tracy and Mike crush us like a milk carton, 35–26. Still, when we come together to shake hands with the teenagers for a good game, I can tell that the tension has eased and we truly do feel like a team.

"The court's all yours," Julie tells Tracy and Mike.

As the teenagers take the court, Julie and I wave good-bye to T. J. and Stinger and start walking back toward Gladrags.

"Hey, Albright! Wait up!" Stinger calls, and runs to catch up with us with T. J. at his heels. "I—I should have passed to you guys sooner. If I had, we could've given Tracy and Mike a run for their money."

T. J. nudges Stinger. "What'd I tell you, man? She really can play."

Stinger looks down and digs the toe of his gym shoe into the ground. "You're right," he says. "The Jaguars could really use a player like you."

Julie beams, her eyes sparkling with gratitude. "Thanks, Stinger."

As we walk back to Gladrags, I can see that Stinger's words really made a difference. Now Julie has a spring in her step that was missing before,

when she was feeling down about everything.

I think about how much Julie has had to go through to get people to believe in her as a basketball player—the petition, the HORSE game, the scrimmage against the teenagers—and how even she lost hope for a little while, because of the attitudes of people like that Coach Manley and boys like Stinger. Then I think of Chloe encouraging me to join the basketball team earlier today. She believes in me, and my team back home did, too. There's nothing stopping *me* from trying out for the team—nothing but my own lack of confidence.

When we reach Gladrags, I stop, holding the mood ring tightly in my hand. "Um, Julie? I need to go home now. Good luck with the basketball team—I sure hope you get on."

Julie smiles, then sets the ball under one foot and gives me a hug. "Thanks for your help today. You were a great teammate."

I hug her back. "And Julie, you know what else— I've decided that first thing Monday morning, I'm going to go sign up to play on the basketball team at my school." Who knows, I might meet some

teammates as good as Chloe—or Julie. "And the first basket I make will be for you!"

❀ *The End* ❀

To read this story another way and see how different choices lead to a different ending, turn back to page 79.

From our hiding place, we watch the man turn the basketball around in his hands as if looking for a clue. Then he disappears back inside his house.

"We need to find the boys," I say to Julie. "Without them, that man will think we're just making up a story to avoid getting in trouble ourselves."

Julie heaves a sigh and nods. "I guess it's worth a try."

We take off up the stairs. When we reach the top, we look around. Stinger and T. J. have vanished. We are starting to walk back toward the park when we hear a *pssst* from behind us, and T. J. steps furtively out of a storefront alcove, holding the basketball Stinger retrieved from the courtyard. "Are you okay?" he asks. "Where'd you go? I thought you were right behind us."

"We're fine," Julie says, crossing her arms. "But you and Stinger shouldn't have left us alone back there."

T. J. looks down at his shoes. "I know. I'm sorry. Once I realized you weren't behind us, I tried to convince Stinger to go back and find you, but—"

"Let me guess," I say. "He wouldn't do it."

T. J. shakes his head. "He just ran off. And I was just about to come find you—honest."

"What should we do?" I ask.

T. J. looks up. "Well . . ." he starts and then pauses, as if he's trying to figure out how to say something difficult. "Do we have to *do* anything? I mean, how would he even know it was us?"

I realize he's right. If nobody saw us, we could just walk away and nobody would know. The only thing we'd lose is an old basketball.

Julie seems to be considering this before she takes in a quick breath. "Wait a minute . . ." She grabs the ball from T. J. and frantically turns it around. "This is Stinger's ball."

"So what?" T. J. asks.

"So my ball is the one that broke the window."

"But it wasn't your fault, Julie," I remind her. "If Stinger hadn't—"

Julie interrupts me. "It doesn't matter *whose* fault it is. My ball has my name on it. *J. ALBRIGHT,* in big black letters. My dad made me write my name on it when he got it for me." She gulps. "Really, this

accident has my name written all over it. If anybody's going to get in trouble, it'll be me."

We all fall silent while we think about what this means. I feel a sinking in the pit of my stomach as I replay in my mind the image of the man examining the basketball outside his home. Surely the man has called the police by now, reporting that a J. Albright damaged his property and is now on the loose in San Francisco. And how many J. Albrights can there be in this town?

"I have to go back," Julie says before I can even open my mouth.

T. J. puts his hand on her shoulder. "We'll come with you. We're just as much to blame as you are."

"Yeah," I agree. "We're in this together."

We slowly make our way down the stairs and pause in front of the red and white cottage, not saying a word. I give Julie's hand a squeeze, reassuring her that we are doing the right thing, even though inside my stomach is as fluttery as a leaf in the wind. Arm in arm, and with T. J. right behind us, we march up to the front door and ring the doorbell. The dogs start to bark, which startles me. I had forgotten about the dogs.

The man opens the door. He's frowning. Three dogs are jumping and yapping and pawing at the screen door.

"Cut that out," he orders, shooing them back. He turns to us. "I'm guessing one of you is J. Albright."

Julie swallows hard and steps forward. "That's me," she says. "J for Julie."

"Well, Miss Albright?" he says. "Can you explain to me why I have a basketball in my living room?"

Julie, T. J., and I take turns telling the story, being careful not to leave anything out.

❁ *Turn to page 122.*

run to her. "Julie! Are you okay? What happened? What did Tracy say?"

Julie shakes her head and looks away. "She didn't say anything. She won't even talk to me," she says, taking a shaky, sniffly breath. "She never talks to me about anything. Not the divorce, not moving to a new school, not anything. And now that I have something really important that I need to talk about, she's just shutting me out again. It's like, ever since the divorce, she doesn't have any feelings."

I swallow. *This sounds familiar.* I think back to the conversation—if you can call it that—with Zack in my room this morning.

"I think Tracy and I have something in common," I say, so quietly that Julie has to lean in to hear me over the noise of the arcade games.

"What do you mean?" Julie asks.

I take a deep breath and tell Julie everything. I tell her about our move from Ohio, my parents' separation, my little brother's struggle to adjust to our new life—and my unwillingness to talk to him about it, to share with him how hard it is for me, too. "I thought that a big sister was supposed to stay strong and act

like everything's okay," I explain. "But now that I've gotten to know you, I think I'm starting to understand a little better how a big sister should be."

Julie looks up at me with teary eyes, and suddenly all of my worries about the missing stone fall away. Right now, Julie needs me—and I think I know how to help her.

"Come with me," I tell her, grabbing her hand and leading her back toward the room where she found Tracy just minutes ago.

When Tracy sees us coming, she rolls her eyes in exasperation. "Julie, I told you I don't want to talk about it."

❀ *Turn to page 125.*

A s much as I want to run away, I know that Julie has a good point: It would feel wrong to leave now, even if it means we have to confess without the boys. "Okay," I finally say to Julie. "Let's go talk to the owner of the house."

Julie bobs her head resolutely, and together we step out of the bushes to face the man. He looks up at us and clears his throat.

"Hello, sir," Julie starts. "We're really sorry about your window." We make our way down the stairs as Julie continues. "You see, I should never have suggested to my friends that we play here. I was just trying to—"

"It wasn't her fault," a voice interrupts from the top of the stairs. T. J. runs down the steps to join us in front of the man's house. Stinger is nowhere to be seen.

"This was an accident," T. J. says. And together, Julie, T. J., and I explain the entire story, each of us sharing the blame.

"These are some friends you have here," the man says to Julie.

"Yes, sir," Julie says, hooking our arms in hers.

❀ *Turn to page 122.*

My breath catches in my throat. *I've forgotten what this game was really about.* I challenged the teenagers to a game so that Julie would get the chance to prove to Stinger—and to herself—that she deserves a spot on the basketball team. Instead, I focused on giving Stinger a taste of his own medicine . . . and lost the game for my team in the process.

"Julie, you know that's not true," I tell her. "Boys and girls *can* play together—I mean, just look at Tracy and Mike. They were a good team!" I scan her face for some sign of hope, but she just looks completely dejected. In desperation, I turn to the boys. "Right?"

At first Stinger just crosses his arms tighter across his chest, but when he sees the look in T. J.'s eyes, he softens. "She's right," he says, his voice almost a whisper. "We just got carried away is all."

I nod. "Listen, Julie, our *team* didn't lose the game. Stinger and I did. I'm really sorry."

We're all silent for a moment. Then, "I am, too," says Stinger. He gives Julie a crooked smile. "You're a—a solid player, Julie. You would be a good Jaguar."

Stinger's words hang in the air for an awkward moment. Julie and T. J. look at each other, as if they

can't believe what they just heard. Stinger blushes and quickly changes the subject. "Hey, Hula Hoop," he says, looking me right in the eye now. He snatches the ball from Julie and bounces it to me. "Show us that Hula Hoop move again, will ya?"

I pass the ball behind my back and twirl around, showing off my signature move. Then Stinger tries it, and Julie and T. J. After a few minutes, even Tracy and Mike are spinning and twirling around the court, trying to learn the move, too, with me giving everyone pointers on when to turn and when to jump.

Julie catches my eye, and when I see the sparkle back in her eyes, I'm so glad I decided to say what I did about why we lost the game, even though it wasn't easy to admit. It feels so much better to be laughing and working together than pulling in opposite directions.

"Good one!" I tell Julie, as she sends the ball swishing through the basket. I grab the ball as it falls and toss it to Stinger. "You can really rock that Hula Hoop! Listen, it's time for me to go, but I bet that you'll be teaching the Hula Hoop to the rest of the Jaguar team really soon."

She grins and gives me a quick hug. Then she turns and darts playfully after Stinger, trying to steal the ball.

That's my last sight of her as I leave the park. Finding a hidden spot behind some bushes, I quickly slip on the mood ring, and before I know it, I'm back home.

❁ *The End* ❁

To read this story another way and see how different choices lead to a different ending, turn back to page 69.

swallow hard and join Julie. Together, we walk toward Tracy, who is standing with Mike in front of a strange game that looks like a grandfather clock. At the bottom of the machine it says *Test Your Love.* Just as Julie opens her mouth to signal our presence, the machine seems to come alive. Lightbulbs flash, bells ring, and horns beep. When the alarms and flashing stop, the words HOT STUFF glow red. Mike turns to Tracy with mock surprise while Tracy's cheeks turn a deep pink.

When Tracy sees us, she smiles and acts as if nothing's wrong. "Hey, are you guys all done with that beach cleanup?" she asks.

Julie crosses her arms and says, "Like you care."

But Tracy doesn't seem to hear her. She's too busy giggling with Mike as they move on to the next arcade game.

Julie presses her lips into a thin line. "Tracy!" she barks.

Tracy gives Mike an apologetic smile and then whips around, hissing through her teeth, "Julie, don't make a scene." She nods her head toward Mike and glares at her little sister as if to say, *You had better not*

embarrass me in front of him. Then, in a sugary-sweet voice, she says, "Hey, remember that time Dad took us here to eat, and we had that super fancy lunch and you ordered lobster?"

I see what Tracy's doing—she's trying to change the subject and distract Julie from what's upsetting her, just as I did this morning with Zack when I spotted the bulldog. It's exactly what I do to my brother when I don't want to talk about something difficult. I thought I could help him feel better by switching the conversation to talk about happy things. But now I realize that I wasn't helping *him* at all—I was helping *myself*, by avoiding facing a hard truth. And by dismissing Zack's feelings as if they didn't mean anything, I was just making him feel worse.

Julie's lip quivers, and I can see that she's holding back tears. Tracy quickly looks away and says, "And do you remember when we—"

"Stop!" I shout.

Julie and Tracy—and even Mike—look at me with eyes as wide as half-dollars.

❀ *Turn to page 125.*

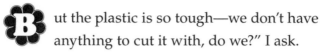

ut the plastic is so tough—we don't have anything to cut it with, do we?" I ask.

Julie rummages through her pockets and pulls out a gum wrapper, a happy-face sticker, and a Kennedy half-dollar, just like the one I found in the window seat.

That's it! I dig into my pocket and feel the peace-sign earring, the 1966 quarter, the flower-power necklace charm from Gladrags, and finally—yes!—the nail clipper that I found among the other treasures in the window seat.

I twist it open and use it to gently cut away the band around the otter's neck. Then I hand the clipper over to Julie, and she snips the band at his feet. He's free, but he seems weak, just lying there in the water, as if he's exhausted by his struggle. Julie grabs a piece of driftwood and uses it to steady him as the waves continue to roll in. The otter clings to it and doesn't try to escape into the open water.

Finally, after what seems like an eternity, two women come running over, each wearing a shirt that says *Animal Rescue*, and name tags that say *Amy* and *Paula*. Julie and I introduce ourselves and explain what happened as Amy pulls on rubber gloves and

lifts the baby otter out of the water.

Paula shakes her head when we show her the plastic rings. "I wish people wouldn't litter like this. Don't they realize that it can have disastrous effects on wildlife?"

Amy checks the otter for other injuries. "He doesn't have any cuts, and he feels well fed, but he's probably chilled." She turns to Julie and me. "Looks like he got separated from his mother somehow. It's a good thing you found him when you did. I'm not sure how much longer he would have lasted once the tide came in."

Paula stands by with a towel. Amy sets the baby otter in Paula's arms, and she wraps him up carefully. "That was smart of you to send someone to get help. You did a real kindness for this little pup," she says.

We gaze down at the fuzzy creature in Paula's arms. He blinks his dark eyes at us and twitches his licorice-jelly-bean nose. He is so cute! As he warms up, he starts making tiny whistles and yelps.

"He's so squeaky!" I say with a big smile.

Julie giggles. "That should be his name. Let's call him Squeaky."

"We have to remember that Squeaky is still a wild animal," Amy reminds us. "We can't let him get too used to humans, since he has to be returned to his natural habitat as soon as possible."

Julie and I understand. As much as we'd like more time with the pup, we know that the sooner he can get back to the ocean, the better. We follow Paula and Amy, heading down to a clear spot on the beach where Squeaky can have plenty of space to test his strength in the water.

When we get to the surf's edge, Paula sets the towel down gently, and Amy unwraps it to let Squeaky reenter the water at will. When the next wave rolls in, Squeaky seems hesitant to dive in. He sniffs the air and then lets out a squeal.

"Is he scared?" Julie asks.

"Maybe a little," Paula replies. "But that squeal was a call to his mother. If she responds, he'll feel much more confident about going back in the water to reach her."

"Eeeeeee!" Squeaky screeches again.

We all wait impatiently for his mother's answer.

Then we hear it—an urgent bark coming from the

water a distance away. Paula pulls out her binoculars and trains them on the water, scanning the waves for an adult sea otter.

Nothing happens at first. Then Squeaky stretches his neck out and lets out another cry.

Paula says, "There she is! I see a head bobbing in the waves."

Julie and I gasp. Paula hands us the binoculars, and we each take turns peering through to see the otter. She calls to her pup, floating on her back as the waves send her up and down upon the surface of the water.

Suddenly Squeaky wiggles and squirms off the towel. Using his back legs and tail, he scoots toward the water, arching his back and then pushing forward toward the surf. Squeaks, squawks, and screeches fill the air as mother and baby sea otter call back and forth. As he dives into the water, another wave comes in, pushing him back onto the sand.

Julie winces. "Will he be strong enough to break through the waves to get to his mama?" she asks.

"I hope so," Amy says. "If not, we're here to help him."

As the wave pulls back, Squeaky tries again. He

swims out past the first break of waves, and then the next.

"Yay, Squeaky!" Julie and I cheer, jumping up and down. Julie and I watch in amazement as the otter pup glides sleekly through the water, riding the wave out to his mother. We take turns with Paula's binoculars, watching as Squeaky greets and nuzzles his mother. Before we know it, mother sea otter is floating on her back, with Squeaky nestled against her chest, nose to nose. We wave good-bye, missing him already.

Silent and content, we pick up our garbage bags and make our way back to the parking lot. As we walk across the beach, we can see what a difference we and the other volunteers have made. It looks like an entirely different beach from the one we arrived at a few hours ago. Grinning at Julie, I slip off my shoes, and she does the same. Seagulls soar overhead, squawking to one another before they alight along the shore. I think of how many beach and sea animals we have helped by cleaning up the litter.

When I get home, I'm going to take Zack to Ocean Beach. I'll tell him how important it is to keep it clean,

so that animals can have a safe place to live and people can continue to enjoy the beach fifty years in the future.

❀ *The End* ❀

To read this story another way and see how different choices lead to a different ending, turn back to page 19.

ulie says, "We're so sorry this happened, Mister—"

"Watson. Douglas Watson."

Julie shakes his hand and introduces T. J. and me. "Mr. Watson, we promise to make this right. We'll do anything!"

"Well, I certainly can't expect kids your age to pay for the damage," Mr. Watson says, his voice starting to soften. "But I'm afraid I *will* have to call your parents."

My heart momentarily sinks. I'm starting to wonder what I can possibly tell him when he asks for my parents' phone number—when Julie speaks up.

"Actually," she says sweetly, "I was wondering if maybe there's anything we could do to help out? You know, like some chores?"

The man looks at his three dogs and smiles to himself. "It's almost a shame this didn't happen an hour earlier. I just got done giving them a bath—not an easy task for one person, you can bet." All three dogs' ears perk up as if they know he's talking about them.

"I imagine one person walking three dogs wouldn't be easy either," Julie says. "How many walks

would it take to pay for the cost of your broken window? We live nearby—we could come as often as you need."

Mr. Watson scratches his chin as he considers Julie's offer. "I suppose a month of walks would do it. Daily, or whenever you're available. Just call before you come over."

"It's a deal!" T. J. says. "And we'll start right now."

The dogs trail behind Mr. Watson as he goes inside to fetch their leashes. When he returns, we help him clip the leads on the dogs' collars while he introduces them. I take hold of Queenie, a peppy Jack Russell terrier, while T. J. takes Trix, the floppy-eared dachshund.

"And this is Mr. Tuxedo," Mr. Watson says, handing the last leash to Julie before scratching the Boston terrier behind the ears. "Watch out for this guy. He may be small, but he's a feisty one."

As if on cue, Mr. Tuxedo lunges forward, pulling Julie toward the stairs. T. J. and I laugh as we follow behind.

"Good luck, kids," Mr. Watson calls to us.

"Thanks," we yell back.

Once Julie gains some control over Mr. Tuxedo, she tells us how relieved she is that Mr. Watson was so understanding.

"I just feel bad that Stinger's not here to do his part," says T. J.

"Well, maybe we can get him to help us on the next walk," says Julie as Mr. Tuxedo surges ahead again, nearly pulling her over. "But let's give Mr. Tuxedo to Stinger next time," she calls over her shoulder as the dog hauls her down the sidewalk.

T. J. and I laugh and walk faster to catch up with her. After several blocks, we loop back and finally start back up the stairs. Mr. Watson greets us at the landing in front of his house. "Welcome back," he says. "There's someone here who has something to say to you."

❁ *Turn to page 129.*

take a deep breath and step up to Tracy.

"Tracy, Julie really needs to talk to you."

"What is there to say?" Tracy snaps. "I'm done talking about Mom and Dad."

I glance at Julie, and then turn back to Tracy. "I get that it's hard to talk about this kind of family stuff. But Julie's your sister—she needs you."

Tracy looks as if she's not sure what to say. She crosses her arms in front of her and glares at her sister.

I lean in and whisper, "Go ahead, Julie. Tell her what's on your mind."

Julie starts out slowly. "You've changed lately. The old Tracy would never have asked me to lie. But now you're lying to Mom and you want me to lie for you, too. And you act like it's nothing."

Tracy looks at Mike and gives him an embarrassed half-smile. When she turns back to Julie, she seems to be pleading with her eyes for her to stop.

But Julie continues. "Then you and Mike pretend that you did all this work to help clean up the beach. You lie about it just to get your paper signed, when you know very well that the only work you did was on your tan."

"Come on, Julie," Tracy says. "That was just—"

But in a gush of words, all of Julie's pent-up feelings of hurt and anger and confusion come pouring out. "You've been acting so different since the divorce. You never come with me to see Dad on the weekends. Did you ever stop to consider how that makes *him* feel? Or *me*?"

Tracy throws up her hands in exasperation. "Do you think Dad ever considered how *we* felt when he and Mom divorced? It's never going to be the same again, so why even try? The life we had before as a family is gone, Julie."

Julie's eyes tear up. She looks stunned, as if Tracy just slapped her. "Tracy, we're still a family," she whispers. "Just because things are different doesn't mean Dad doesn't love us. I still love him, and Mom, and you, because you're still my family. Right?"

Tracy shrugs. "The truth is, it just doesn't feel that way to me right now. I'm sorry, but I can't fake it."

"Nobody's asking you to fake anything, Tracy! But I am asking you to stop lying," Julie begs. "Please, Tracy—don't you have any feelings at all?"

"What do you know about it?" Tracy says, shaking her head. "You're just a kid."

I can't help wincing when I hear that. I had that
same thought when Zack was trying to talk to me
this morning. Even though this conversation is about
Julie's family, not mine, I realize I might have something to contribute. Steeling my courage, I speak up.
"Julie knows a lot, Tracy. Just because she's younger
doesn't mean her feelings don't count." Thinking
of my little brother, I try to find the right words.
"Sometimes, maybe the younger you are, the more
clearly you can see things—and then face them
head-on."

I squeeze Julie's hand and look her in the eye.
"And Julie, just because Tracy has trouble talking about
things doesn't mean she has no feelings. Actually, I bet
she has more feelings than she can handle, so many
that she can't fit any more feelings—even yours—into
her heart, because it hurts too much."

No one says a word. Even the noise of the arcade
doesn't seem to penetrate the silence that surrounds
our little group. Mike and I look on as Julie and Tracy
face each other, speechless.

Finally Julie takes a step toward her sister and
speaks. "I . . . I'm sorry, Tracy." She looks up, tears on

her cheeks. "I want to be able to talk to you, because you're my sister and you understand things better than anybody. But . . . I can't if you keep lying to me about stuff. Or if you're not there."

Tracy turns away and swipes at her own eyes. Then she nods and reaches for her sister, folding Julie into a hug.

❁ *Turn to page 132.*

o our surprise, from behind Mr. Watson steps Stinger, his eyes glued to the ground. "I shouldn't have bailed on you guys," he mumbles. "It wasn't fair to leave you all here, when it was really my fault to begin with. I'm sorry it took me so long to come back. I went home to break open my piggy bank." He stuffs his hand into his pocket and pulls out four crumpled dollar bills. "Here," he says, handing the money to Mr. Watson. "This is to help pay for the window."

"That's really boss, Stinger," Julie says. "Thank you."

Stinger reddens. "I know it's not enough, but—"

"It's plenty," Mr. Watson says, patting Stinger on the back. He gathers the leashes from us and smiles at his dogs, which have quieted down considerably after our long walk. "Thanks, kids. I appreciate your taking responsibility for the window. See you again soon."

We thank Mr. Watson and give the dogs a good-bye pat before turning to go. Mr. Watson clears his throat. We turn around to see him holding up Julie's ball. "Next time, don't let this get away from you!" He tosses it to us.

Julie catches it and holds it close to her chest. "I won't, I promise."

When we reach the top of the steps, Stinger looks at Julie sheepishly. "It took some serious guts to own up to that guy after breaking his window." He gives her a friendly punch on the arm and says, "You know what, Albright? You're not so bad—I mean . . . for a girl."

Julie nudges him softly with her elbow, and the boys turn to leave. During the short walk back to Gladrags, Julie and I are nearly giddy about our remarkable day. I think about how proud I feel that we were all able to come together to fix the problem, instead of running away from it.

That's when I realize how often I run away from the problems in my own life. Just this morning, I refused to talk to Zack about the things that are troubling both of us. And then I avoided the subject of joining the basketball team when I spoke with Chloe—just because I was afraid of not being good enough to try out. I realize I want to be more like Julie, who faces everything head-on—by starting a petition, by proving herself to others, and by admitting when she's in the wrong. When I get home, I'm going to sit down and have a good talk with Zack. Then I'm going to go to school on Monday and sign up for that basketball team.

Before I know it, Julie and I are standing in front of Gladrags. Julie squeezes me into a tight hug. "Thank you for being there for me today," she says. "Maybe we can play another game of HORSE sometime soon. You can teach me that far-out Hula Hoop move."

"And you can teach me speed dribbles." I stop and wince. "As long as we stay far away from stairs."

Julie giggles. "Absolutely."

As she walks into Gladrags, I call to her. "Good luck, Julie."

She grins, and the door closes behind her.

I step to the front door of Julie's apartment building and look around to make sure nobody is looking. I twist the mood ring on my finger and—*whoosh!*—I land on my window seat in my room. I look at the clock on my computer. It's still 12:35, the perfect time to sit down and talk to Zack. The perfect time to start facing my life head-on.

❁ *The End* ❁

To read this story another way and see how different choices lead to a different ending, turn back to page 19.

Tracy kisses the top of Julie's head. Then she pulls a folded paper out of the back pocket of her jeans and rips it in half. She gives one half to Julie and the other to me.

When I open my half, I see that it's the form for Tracy's community service project, with Chip's and Kimberly's names signed at the bottom.

"Hey!" Mike objects, but then he thinks better of it and lets out a heavy sigh.

"There's still a lot of beach left to clean," Tracy says to Mike. "Let's get back out there and do it for real this time."

Mike nods and gives Julie an apologetic smile.

Tracy looks at Julie and says, "Just hold on to those papers until I see you tonight."

"But I'll be at Dad's tonight—" Julie starts and then takes in a quick breath. "Wait. Are you saying you'll come to Dad's?"

Tracy nods. "But you have to promise me you and Dad will make your famous strawberry French toast."

"Of course!" Julie says, throwing her arms around her sister again.

Tracy laughs. "I would have gone even without the

promise of strawberry French toast. I think I might have left some stuff in my old room anyway—I can't find my favorite earrings anywhere."

Julie blushes. "Um, Tracy? I might have something to do with that. I . . . I sort of borrowed them and—" Julie stammers as Tracy crosses her arms, waiting for her to spit it out. "—I didn't return them because, well, I think I might have lost one."

"First you borrowed them without asking, and then you lost one?" Tracy says in disbelief. "Julie, you know those peace-sign earrings are my favorite."

Julie shrinks at Tracy's words, and I wish there was something—anything—I could do to ease the tension before it turns into another fight. Then a thought flashes in my head, a vague sense of déjà vu that slowly transforms into a real memory in my head. I dig into my pocket and fish out the peace-sign earring that I found inside the window seat in my—and Julie's—room.

"Um, Julie?" I hold out the earring in my palm. "Is this it?"

Julie looks at me incredulously. "How did you get that?"

"I, um, found it," I say, not wanting to lie but

avoiding the whole truth. "Just before I met you at Gladrags."

"Thanks!" Tracy says, and then she gives Julie a forgiving hair-ruffle. "Just ask permission next time, Jules."

Julie nods gratefully. Then her eyes land on the floor next to my feet. "What's that?" She leans down to pick something up before jiggling it in the palm of her hand. "It must have fallen out of your pocket when you pulled out the earring."

I gasp. "It's the stone from my mood ring!"

I had completely forgotten about it until now. It's almost as if the stone hid itself from me until I had helped Julie and Tracy reunite. But how did it end up in my pocket in the first place? All sorts of impossible scenarios go through my head before I remember the moment I reached into my pocket for the quarter to put into the fortune-teller machine. The stone must have come loose from the setting while my hand was in my pocket.

Julie hands the stone to me nonchalantly, having no sense of its value. I press it back into the setting and use a fingernail to push the prong back into place.

Now that my ring is in one piece, I realize I had better
return home before I lose the stone for good.

We follow Mike and Tracy outside, and Julie
hands them her last garbage bags and the two pairs
of rubber gloves. Then, with a wave, Tracy and Mike
head toward the beach.

On the ride back to Gladrags, I think about how
to be a better big sister to Zack. It means being less
moody and selfish, listening to him and not dismissing
his fears, and answering his questions the best I can.
It means spending more time with him when we're
missing our old home back in Ohio—or missing Dad.

When we arrive at Gladrags, I tell Julie that it's
time for me to go, and wrap her in a good-bye hug.
"Maybe I'll see you at the beach someday," I tell her.

"I'd love that," she says. "Thank you. For everything." She gives me one last glowing smile before
disappearing into her mom's store.

I make my way down the sidewalk, my heart full
of this amazing, unforgettable day. As soon as I round
the corner, I sit down on the curb, steadying myself. I
hold out my hand and gaze at the mood ring, the ring
that brought me here, the ring that connects me to

Julie. The ring that's my way back to family and home. The stone gradually changes color before my eyes, turning from amber to green to sky blue. I'm not sure what blue means, but I know how I feel: I feel calm, peaceful . . . happy.

At long last, I close my eyes and slip the mood ring from my finger.

❀ *The End* ❀

To read this story another way and see how different choices
lead to a different ending, turn back to page 45.

ABOUT Julie's Time

In Julie's day, many people were like the basketball coach at her school: They viewed athletics as an activity for boys and men only. Girls were expected to sit on the sidelines and cheer. Some schools didn't even have gym classes for girls. Girls like Julie who wanted to play sports were out of luck.

But people's attitudes about sports were beginning to change. When Bobby Riggs, a male tennis pro, bragged that a man could beat any woman on the tennis court, a female pro named Billie Jean King accepted his challenge in a match that became known as "The Battle of the Sexes." Billie Jean King knew that if she lost, it would confirm what a lot of people thought: that females shouldn't be taken seriously as athletes. So she prepared hard for the match, and as millions of people watched on TV, she creamed Bobby Riggs in three straight sets, sending a powerful message that female athletes could play sports just as well as men.

A woman in Congress, Edith Green, wanted to make sure that girls would have the same opportunities boys had at school—and that included playing sports. When Congress passed a law known as the Education Amendments of 1972, Edith Green included a section forbidding *sex discrimination,* or unequal treatment of boys and girls, at schools that received money from the federal government—which included nearly every school in the country, from elementary to college. This section became known as Title Nine.

It requires schools to provide athletic teams for girls, or else let girls play on the boys' teams. Thanks to women like Edith Green, Billie Jean King, and many other women's rights activists—as well as aspiring athletes like Julie—millions of girls today are athletes and play on sports teams.

Another issue that people were gaining new awareness of in the 1970s was the environment. Americans were starting to understand that nature—the plants and animals, the air and water—needed protection from human activity. People formed organizations and raised money to clean up lakes and rivers, beaches, and other natural areas. In 1972, Congress passed the Endangered Species Act, making it illegal to harm endangered animals and plants or to disturb their habitats.

California sea otters, like the one Julie helped rescue, were nearing extinction in 1977 when they were listed as threatened under the Endangered Species Act. But through the efforts of conservationists and wildlife biologists, the California sea otter is making a comeback, and today there are almost 2,800 sea otters living along California's coastline.

The 1960s and '70s, when Julie was a girl, are famous for social activism. When people looked around and saw problems in the world, they got others involved. They marched in the streets and lobbied Congress to pass new laws. They wanted to make America a better, safer, fairer place—for all people and for all living things.

Read more of JULIE'S stories,
available from booksellers and at *americangirl.com*

❀ *Classics* ❀
Julie's classic series, now in two volumes:

Volume 1:
The Big Break
Julie's parents' divorce means a new home, a new school, and new friends. Will Julie ever feel at home in her new life?

Volume 2:
Soaring High
As Julie begins to see that change can bring new possibilities, she sets out to make some big changes of her own!

❀ *Journey in Time* ❀
Travel back in time and spend a day with Julie!

A Brighter Tomorrow
Step back into the 1970s and help Julie win her basketball game, save a stranded sea otter, and clean up the beach! Choose your own path through this multiple-ending story.

❀ *Mysteries* ❀
More thrilling adventures with Julie!

Lost in the City
Julie's taking care of a valuable parrot—and it's disappeared.

The Silver Guitar
A guitar from a famous rock star leads Julie and T. J. into danger.

The Puzzle of the Paper Daughter
A note written in Chinese leads Julie on a search for a long-lost doll.

The Tangled Web
Julie meets a new friend who isn't who she seems to be.

✿ *A Sneak Peek at* ✿

The Big Break
A Julie Classic

Volume 1

What happens to Julie?
Find out in the first volume of her classic stories.

ey, Julie!" T. J. called, slamming his locker shut from across the hall. "Coach Manley is posting the basketball sign-up sheet after school today."

In her excitement over Career Day, Julie had forgotten that today was the day for basketball team sign-ups. She hadn't even remembered to ask Mom about it. Julie could hardly sit still, waiting for the final bell to ring. As soon as school was out, she rushed down the hall toward the coach's office.

"No running in the halls, young lady!" called Principal Sanchez. "Even after school." Julie forced herself to slow down.

Coach Manley was a gym teacher. He had buzz-cut hair like a G. I. Joe, a growly face, and a thick neck. Every time Julie passed the gym, he was always shouting.

Julie looked for a sign-up sheet on the wall but didn't see one. She summoned her courage and knocked on the coach's door. She knew just how Dorothy felt knocking at the door of the Wizard of Oz.

"Enter," barked the coach.

Julie fixed on the bump in his nose to steady herself.

He reminded her of a dragon, about to breathe fire.

"Hi, Mr. Manley," she said. "My name's Julie. Julie Albright. I'm a fourth grader, and—"

"Yeah, yeah. You looking for the sign-up sheets? Got 'em right here."

"Really? That's great! So I'm the first one?"

"Yep. How many dozen should I put you down for?" asked Coach Manley.

"Dozen? Dozen what?"

"Cookies. For the basketball bake sale," said the coach, leaning back in his chair. "We're trying to raise money for new uniforms. How about I put you down for some chocolate chip cookies. My favorite."

"Cookies? I'm not here about cookies," said Julie. "I'm here about the team. I want to be *on* the team. The basketball team."

"We don't have a girls' team at Jack London Elementary. We can barely afford the boys' team. Why do you think we're having a bake sale?"

Julie took a deep breath. "Not the girls' team. The boys' team."

Coach Manley sat up. She had his full attention now. "Let me get this straight," he said slowly. "You

want *me* to put *you* on the boys' basketball team."

Julie nodded, her heart pounding.

Coach Manley smiled and shook his head. "Young lady, the basketball team is for boys, and boys only. Got that?"

"I'm as good as the boys," Julie said softly. "Just give me a chance to try out. Please."

"Sorry. Answer's N-O, no. This is my team and I make the rules. When spring rolls around, we'll have some intramural games—softball, tetherball, badminton. Maybe you can play one of those."

Julie shook her head. "That's not the same." She flushed and looked down at the floor, embarrassed to meet his eyes. A strange new feeling washed over her. It felt like a mixture of shame, frustration, and an emotion she couldn't quite identify.

She glanced up at the coach. He had turned back to his desk, signaling that it was time for her to leave. Her instinct was to run out of his office and never see him again. But something kept her feet firmly planted to the floor.

Finally, Coach Manley looked up. "I have work to do. This conversation is finished."

Julie felt her insides go all runny, like the yellow belly of a breakfast egg. As she turned to go, hot tears smarted at the back of her eyes. Julie swallowed hard, pushing back her fear.

"If there's not a basketball team for girls at this school, you have to let a girl play on the boys' team," she told the coach, her voice shaking. "I read it in the newspaper."

"Did the paper say I don't have to do anything I don't want to do? Case closed. Out of my office."

"It's the law!" Julie whispered, backing away.

"Well, I have a news flash for you, young lady. In this gym, I'm the law." Coach Manley towered over Julie as he leaned across the desk toward her. "Now, do I have to call the principal to escort you out of here? Or will you leave on your—"

Julie didn't wait to hear the rest. She fled. She ran all the way home, wind biting her ears and stinging her cheeks.

At Gladrags, Mom and Tracy had newspaper spread across the table and counter in the back, and

they were gluing beads and buttons onto blank white lampshades.

"Hi, honey," said Mom. "I was telling your sister all about Career Day. You just missed some girls from your class. I've already had three new customers since my talk today."

Julie wondered if they were the Water Fountain Girls. "That's great, Mom."

"What's wrong with you?" asked Tracy. "Your face is as red as a beet!"

"Wait!" said Julie, looking at the table where they were working. "Are these all the newspapers from last week? Thursday or Friday? I have to find something!" she said frantically, lifting up corners of the newspaper and peering at headlines. "Here it is!" She flipped the paper over to the inside of the sports section, careful to avoid getting stuck with glue, and pointed to the headline: "High School Girl Tackles Boys, School Board."

"See? This girl wasn't allowed to play on the school football team, so she went to court. She won, and they had to let her play, because of this new law."

"Oh, yeah. We learned about that in civics class,"

said Tracy. "They passed some big federal law to make things more equal."

"I believe it's called Title Nine," said Mom. "But what does this have to do with you, Julie?"

"It's the basketball coach at school," Julie explained. "He won't let me play on the team because I'm a girl."

"He's a male chauvinist pig," said Tracy.

"Tracy!" Mom sounded a little shocked. "Where did you hear that?"

"Some people in tennis called Bobby Riggs a male chauvinist pig because he thought Billie Jean King couldn't beat him," Tracy replied. "Then she trounced him in a big match and proved that girls can be just as good as boys in sports."

"Look, honey," said Mom, smoothing out Julie's hair. "I don't see why you shouldn't be allowed to play on the team, if that's what you really want. Let's talk this over with your dad when he gets back next week."

"I already talked to Dad about it, and even *he* doesn't want me to play on the boys' team," Julie told her. "But they don't have a girls' team. Besides, tryouts for all the positions are this week. Next week will be too late."

Julie grabbed the page with the article and rushed up to her room. She scooped up her basketball and bounced it against the wall. *Thwump! Thwump!* She knew Mom didn't like her bouncing it in the house, but the satisfying thump of the ball helped ease the bundled-up feelings inside her.

Nobody ever asked her what *she* wanted. Divorce. *Thwump.* Moving. *Thwump.* Changing schools and leaving Ivy. *Thwump-thwump-thwump!* This morning, her horoscope had said "Create your own future by taking charge." Well, taking charge was what she was *trying* to do.

Julie stopped bouncing the ball and sat up straight. She wasn't going to give up. And they couldn't make her!

The rest of the week at school seemed to drag on forever. On Friday, Julie was standing in front of her locker at the end of the day when she overheard the Water Fountain Girls whispering to each other.

"Shh! There she is. She's the one," said Alison.

"The one what?" asked Angela. Or was it Amanda?

"Can you believe it?" said Alison. "She actually asked Coach Manley if she could be on the *boys'* basketball team!"

"She's a TOMBOY!" Amanda and Angela hissed, saying the word too loud on purpose.

Julie froze. She stuck her head deeper into her locker, pretending to look for her reading workbook. A voice came up behind her. "Just ignore them. You're good at basketball."

Julie pulled her head out of her locker and smiled gratefully at T. J. "Does Coach Manley already have his team picked out?" she asked.

"Nope. He's still choosing positions. I'm keeping my fingers crossed I'm a starter. Wish me luck."

"Luck," Julie said longingly, waving good-bye to T. J.

About the Author

MEGAN McDONALD grew up in a house full of books and sisters—four sisters, who inspire many of the stories she writes. She has loved to write since she was ten, when she got her first story published in her school newspaper. Megan vividly remembers growing up in the 1970s, from making apple-seed bracelets to learning the metric system. San Francisco is close to home for Megan, who lives with her husband in Sebastopol, California, where she writes the Judy Moody series and many other books for young people.